Other Erotic Tales by Laura Baumbach

A Bit of Rough
Details of the Hunt
Roughhousing
Mexican Heat
Walk Through Fire
Enthralled
Sin and Salvation

Coming Soon:

The Lost Temple of Karttikeya
Genetic Snare
Entranced
Monster
Ripples on the Moon

Copyright 2007 by Laura Baumbach

Published by MLR Press, LLC
3052 Gaines Waterport Rd.
Albion, NY 14411
Cover Art by Lorraine Brevig
Editing by Sue H.

Printed in the United States of America.

ISBN# 0-9793110-0-4
ISBN# 978-0-9793110-0-0

Second Edition
2007

Out There in the Night

Chapter One

Kenai Peninsula, Alaska – January 5, 1905

The arctic night was so black and crisp, Adam Lowell felt like he could reach out and actually touch it. The winds picked up the icy snow and swirled clouds of needle-sharp, white crystals through the bitter air, nearly obscuring the small clearing he had chosen for his campsite.

Adam pulled the thick bearskin robe tightly around his broad shoulders and hunkered down by the fire. With the help of the stiff breeze, his long, straight hair pulled free of its usual leather tie, cascading past his shoulders like a black waterfall. Gusts of wind made the thick hair dance around his face, first obliterating, then accenting his sharp facial features.

First-born son of German trapper Frank Lowell and his beautiful native Alaskan wife Wenona, Adam was a striking man. At six foot four, two hundred and forty pounds, he was the embodiment of a dark Dena'ina warrior the likes of which had not been seen for several generations. A combination of the best of both his parents, Adam had his father's towering build, enduring strength and quick intelligence. He also possessed his mother's sharp-boned, dark good looks, honed survival instincts, and, as he was finding out in recent months, her spiritual link to her ancient fore-fathers.

Since the first full moon of this year, Adam's thirty-fifth year of life, spiritwalkers had visited his dreams more nights than not. Despite his father's attempts to isolate him from his mother's heritage, Adam found himself uncontrollably drawn to his native Indian culture. Especially on the nights like tonight, when the winds called and the moon shone full and bright. Tonight the moon had a rusty orange veil over it Adam had never seen before. He basked in the light, its hazy glow warming his spirit.

The winds beckoned him, stirring his blood like they stirred the restless snows now swirling around his head. They made him leave the comfort and safety of his father's settlement, luring him farther and farther into the frozen night and the dangers of the untamed wilderness that surrounded his world. Tonight the winds said they were summoning him home, a home Adam had never seen.

A natural born hunter, an experienced predator of the less skilled and weaker species that inhabited his territory, Adam preferred to hunt at night, stalking the stalkers -- the foraging bear, the sly wild cat, the roving wolf. Many of the prize pelts his father's trading store sold were the results of his nights spent on the prowl by moonlight. On these special nights, Adam was at the top of his game. Nothing escaped his rifle's sights. He was the ultimate primal hunter, winds in his face and senses honed.

But tonight, the winds sang a new tune in his

ears. Orange moonbeams illuminating his path, leading him deeper and deeper into the frozen tundra, Adam was pulled past the borders of familiar territory farther than he had ever traveled before. Tonight, Adam felt the call of the spiritwalkers.

Respectful of the spirit world and the demands of the Ancient Ones, Adam took care in choosing a clearing to take his rest. There he built a small fire and waited for the anticipated dream-quest he instinctively knew would descend upon him. Just before midnight, a heavy exhaustion clouded his mind and drained his usually substantial strength. He let the creeping lethargy claim him and sleep swiftly followed. Crouched low by the sputtering fire, tucked deep into the folds of his thick bearskin robe, surrounded by miles of glacial fields devoid of other human life, Adam Lowell began to dream.

In his dream, Adam became his spirit totem, the gray wolf. A huge, black-coated animal, long-legged, with rusty orange eyes, the color of this night's foreboding moon. The only vestige of his human form still present were the two silver bands braided into his long black fur on the left side of his head. He could feel their weight swing against his face as he ran through the frozen landscape, over hills and into the dense forests of tall trees, spurred on by the instinctive knowledge that something followed close behind.

Eventually, he became aware of several more wolves joining him on the run. The pack came from behind and down the hills on both sides, forming a semi-circle around him, but never out-distancing him or coming up to run neck-and-neck with him. He knew he was the leader of the pack, alpha male, the biggest and strongest.

After what seemed like hours, Adam slowed and the pack responded to his lead, slowing with him, gathering closer until he came to a halt in a small clearing just like the one the human Adam had chosen. The pack groveled and nipped, howling acceptance or half-hearted taunts at him, though no one made a serious gesture to challenge him. Adam suddenly felt a bond of kinship with these animals that his human half-breed spirit had never experienced.

Feeling oddly content with the surreal situation, Adam looked down to study the massive paws in front of him, awed by the size and the power of his new canine form. A beam of rusty moonlight fell across his forelegs. As he watched, his legs stretched and grew, mutating to a bizarre version somewhere between wolf and human. Panting, he raised fur-covered hands to his face to find a snout. It was thickset, sharply angled and covered in short, coarse hair. He sported pointed ears, a thick mane of heavy, protective fur at his neck and teeth that had tripled in size and length. He was morphing once again, from primal wolf to ancient skinwalker.

A sudden chorus of forlorn howls rose up from the surrounding pack. Shocked, Adam's gaze darted up to witness the same transformations occurring all around him as his pack of wolves, male and female alike, changed.

Startled by the too real, blood chilling howls, Adam jarred awake from his dream-quest, panting hard and covered in sweat, happy to be back in the real world. His relief was short-lived. His dream-clouded eyes struggled to focus on his shadow-shrouded surroundings. Once clear, they settled on a pair of rusty-orange, glowing eyes set in a huge, square, black fur-covered face less than a foot away from his own. Before Adam had time to reach for the pistol on his belt, the massive wolf was on him, tearing at the flesh of his arms, shoulders, and finally his neck.

Adam cried out, the pain of the short-lived attack excruciating. He fell to the ground in a heap on the bear robe, his body ravaged, his mind clouded with questions and his life ebbing away.

Around the fire, the nearby shadows danced, and the sound of flutes and drums was carried on the winds. The flames of the fire flared then rose high in the night sky. Adam felt his spirit leave his body and soar up into the air with them. Chanting joined the music and a surge of power tore through Adam's weakening body. Unbridled strength and self-assurance replaced the pain and fear, and a sense of purpose filled Adam's soul as his spirit returned to him.

The last thing the human Adam Lowell saw before he passed out was the creature destined to be a part of him for all time. The black beast that had attacked him was the last of the nearly extinct species of massive gray wolf which scientists call 'canis lupus alces', but was better known in Adam's native culture as skinwalker, or werewolf.

***

Chapter Two

Kenai Peninsula, Alaska – January 1, 2005

The arctic had turned out to be everything Dr. Connor Jacy expected and more. The raw wildness of the land and simple lifestyle of the people, both native Alaskans and Settlers, appealed to a part of the young doctor that was yearning for a less complicated existence.

Connor was a good doctor, very caring and highly skilled. Only five foot seven and one hundred fifty pounds, Connor was small, but well muscled. Active in a number of athletic sports since childhood. He had an endurance that left his less physically fit colleagues in the dust when it came to dealing with the rigors and demands of a hectic medical practice.

By age thirty-two, Connor had already grown tired of the suburban family practice he'd shared with nine other physicians. It had its rewards, but it hadn't turned out to be as satisfying as Connor thought it would be.

He had wanted to be doctor all of his life, but now something inside of him longed for more excitement and adventure. He felt an indefinable urge to leave behind the noise and restrictions of city life. He wanted to explore some of nature's untouched lands.

Connor picked a remote region on the Alaskan peninsula for his first adventure by becoming a member of a traveling health care team. Expert medical care was difficult to find for the remote settlements and the placement firm eagerly welcomed a fit, young, board-certified, licensed physician.

When the handsome and persuasive Dr. Greg Pierce from the Pierce Clinic in Nekenano, Alaska turned on his seductive charm during the placement interview, Connor couldn't find a reason to resist. The frozen wilderness of Alaska would be his starting point. Who knew what wondrous things were waiting for him out there?

Slender, with wavy blond hair and vibrant green eyes, Connor was an attractive man by most standards despite his imperfections. A small, but obvious crescent-shaped scar high up on his left cheek was a lasting testament to a bizarre coffee cup incident when he was eight. Another half-moon scar at the corner of his right eye, gained in a rock climbing accident, added a quirky, off-center crinkle to his boyish face when he smiled. His small, even white teeth, sun-bronzed skin, and strong chin added a healthy exuberance to complete his wholesome look.

Connor preferred worn jeans to crisp dress pants and soft, wrinkled chino shirts to sterile dress shirts and restrictive neckties. He liked comfortable clothes and tough demanding jobs. Connor liked to be challenged by nature and life.

Right now he was being challenged by a different kind of force of nature, his current lover and boss, Dr. Greg Pierce. Head of the medical team at the town's tiny clinic, Greg was also single-handedly responsible for the medical facility's very existence.

Tall, dark, ridiculously rich, and handsome in an old-world Roman way, Greg was used to getting what he wanted. He relentlessly pursued his every desire.

Today, as every other day since the beginning of their relationship five months ago, Dr. Greg Pierce was after the one thing he couldn't have.

"Come on, lover. How do you know you won't like it if you've never tried it?" Greg traced the curve of Connor's small, firm ass and gently massaged the base of his spine, straying toward his intended target.

Connor clenched his ass and rolled away from the seductive caress, well aware of where the questing fingers were headed. It was too early in the morning for this.

"I don't have to have a tent pole shoved up my ass to know I won't like it. The same goes for your cock, Greg. I'm not interested." He pulled a corner of the flannel sheet over his hips and reached for Greg's bobbing, eager erection. He was too tired to talk his way past this old argument. It was easier to distract the man.

In a maneuver accomplished only because he was wiry and quick, Connor lunged up and pinned his taller partner to the bed by the hips. Grinning up from between Greg's now outstretched legs, he blew a stream of warm breath over the man's balls and watched as they tightened in response. His grin widened when Greg sucked in an unwilling breath of anticipation, squirming his ass against the mattress.

"Besides, *lover*, there are more interesting places to put your cock. An ass is just a dry hole, but a mouth," he sucked the dark, full tip of Greg's cock in past his lips and swirled his tongue under the sensitive rim, then popped it out, making a wet, sucking sound. "Is a warm, wet hole with a number," he licked up one side of the curved shaft, "of other," then down, "*assets*."

"Maybe," Greg grunted, "but nothing compares with a tight, hot asshole, Connor. Trust me." Contrary to his words, Greg arched up into Connor's waiting mouth, his voice strained and breathless. Hissing, he reached down and threaded his hands through Connor's blond hair, the longer style Connor had let his hair grow into just the right length for holding onto.

"And trust *me*, Greg, my ass can't do *this*."

Connor ran his lips down the thick shaft, touching every vein and ridge. When he reached the base, he lapped at the wrinkled sac, sucking first one ball, then the other into his mouth. Tugging the thoroughly moistened sac to one side, he snaked his tongue farther back, teasing the pulsing root of his lover's cock where it joined his pelvic floor. Heavy panting and a tighter grip on his head let him know Greg was adequately distracted.

Working his way back to the leaking tip, Connor licked the droplet of white cum from the slit, stabbing the opening with the point of his stiffened tongue. He slowly sucked the head into his mouth again, running the tip of his tongue under the sensitive rim. When Greg groaned and began thrusting his hips, Connor swished a mouthful of slick spit around in his mouth, bathing just the head in the body-hot fluid.

"Jesus, Connor. Suck me!" Greg bucked and thrust, sliding his cock to the back of Connor's throat. "That's it. Do it!"

Tugging firmly on the hair wrapped around his fingers, Greg bobbed Connor's head up and down, easing more of his shaft into Connor's throat.

Gagging slightly, Connor awkwardly rose up on his knees and swallowed down Greg's cock. The blunt tip nudged the back of his soft palate. He changed the angle of his neck to let it slide farther down his throat. The scent of Greg's expensive body gel mingling with the tang of sweat tickled his nose, along with the dark, curly, groin hair. Hollowing his cheeks, Connor sucked hard and worked the muscles of his throat.

He looked up when Greg grunted and pulled his knees up to either side. His gaze met half-lidded hazel eyes, dulled with lust, ravenously taking in his every move.

"Christ, you're good." Greg licked his own dry lips, the tip of his tongue pressed to the outside edge of his top lip. His face was flushed and contorted in a grimace of what appeared to be unattained need.

Connor's free hand immediately went to his own full erection, stroking it in time to Greg's jerky thrusts. He felt the shaft between his swollen lips pulse and he hastened to grip it with both hands. Sliding one sweaty palm from the top to bottom of the meaty cock, he followed it immediately with his other moist hand, repeating the smooth, seamless motion over and over while he sucked on the head. He knew from personal experience this was like sinking into a never-ending, tight, hot tunnel. It was heaven.

"Fuck, fuck, fuck, FUCK!"

Greg must have felt the same. Before Connor was ready, a hot stream of thick, slightly bitter cum hit the roof of his mouth and flowed down his throat. He continued to suck, swallowing the spray, trying to breathe and keep up the rhythm at the same time.

After a few more firm thrusts, the grip in his hair slowly lessened and Connor let Greg's fading erection slip from between his lips with a slight slurping sound. The flaccid shaft fell forward, slapping one hairy thigh. Greg jumped at the impact.

"Easy!"

Releasing Connor's head, Greg tenderly ran his hands down either side of his lover's face. "I'll say this for you, Connor, nobody gives head the way you do."

Smiling like a Cheshire cat, Connor lay back on the bed beside his sated lover, waiting for Greg to return the favor.

"Told you so. No matter how much you want my ass, you're never going to find a tongue up there." He grabbed his own cock and began stroking it to ease the building ache behind his balls. Smirking, he thrust his hips suggestively and added, "Unless it's yours."

Greg shifted to the edge of the bed and sat up, his eyes on the alarm clock on the bedside table. "I still want your ass." He patted Connor's leg, a false solicitous tone to his voice. "But any more discussion about it is going to have to wait. I'm due in a meeting in ten minutes."

Greg sprang from the bed and began collecting his clothes that were strewn around the room. He had been in a hurry to climb into bed with a sleepy Connor, hoping to catch the man in a more receptive mood for his persuasive argument. And one more time, it hadn't worked. He pulled on his pants and clutched his shirt and sweater in his arms. His gaze continued to scan the room looking for something more.

Amazed, Connor pointed to his still hard cock.

"What? *Wait!* One of us isn't done here!"

Greg picked up his boots and searched the floor for his socks, never looking in Connor's direction. "Sorry, lover. You know we've been short staffed since Tom's heart attack sent him back to Jersey. His replacement is due in this morning. He's probably downstairs right now." Greg spied a sock under the bed. He went down on one knee to retrieve it, coming up directly in line with Connor's rock hard cock.

Pushing his shaft toward Greg's face, Connor frowned when his invitation was ignored and Greg stood up.

"Didn't I tell you about this?" Greg backed away and kept moving until his hips made contact with the bedroom door.

Pissed and frustrated, Connor threw one arm over his eyes to block out the sight of the other man's slight smirk. "No, Greg, you didn't mention it." He gave a long-suffering sigh. "If you had, I'd have kicked you out of here the minute you showed up this morning." Feeling used, he added, "If you don't have time to do it right, don't *do* me at all."

"Connor, don't get huffy. It can't always be about you." The false hurt in his voice added just the edge it needed to harden Connor's heart.

"Since when has it *ever* been about me?" Connor didn't have to move his arm from his face to know there was a gleam in Greg's eyes. He could hear it in his voice. This was his little way of making Connor pay for refusing him again. "You're a selfish prick sometimes, Greg."

"I know." Greg sighed dramatically. "It's a

curse. But I've learned to live with it. You should, too."

The sweet, mocking tone grated on Connor's nerves, but he refused to give the man the satisfaction of seeing it.

"If you're not going to help out here, get out." He reached down and began to stroke his cock, thumb circling the head in a leisurely fashion he didn't feel. "I have things to do."

He was almost enjoying himself when a triumphant yell from the doorway made him jerk down his arm and raise his head from the pillow.

"Ah ha! Got you!"

Greg leapt across the room and leaned over Connor, one arm supporting his weight while the other reached up over the naked man's head. The rough denim of Greg's jeans rubbed against Connor's erection, making the younger man jump and hiss.

For a brief moment Connor thought Greg had reconsidered until he saw Greg pull a dark green scarf down off the headboard. It must have landed there in the earlier frenzy to undress. The scarf was made of the softest of cashmere and was Greg's favorite personal possession. He wore it everywhere, even inside.

This close, Connor could see the glint of amusement in Greg's eyes, the gold flecks in the pale hazel more pronounced than usual. The smell of cum and after-shave filled his senses and Connor's cock jerked impatiently in his hand.

Smiling seductively, Greg slowly pulled back, amused eyes locked on Connor's. He pulled the scarf across Connor's chest and down his trunk, teasing over his groin and letting it caress the tip of his straining erection.

His voice a soft, sensual whisper of promise, Greg nodded at the quivering pole between them. "Better take an extra minute, minute and a half, in the shower and do something about that, big guy. Don't want to scare the new help."

With one final tug on the scarf, Greg whipped it from Connor's cock and raced to the door. It slammed shut just as a bed pillow smacked the frame.

"Spiteful bastard!"

Connor's voice sounded hollow and empty. He wondered if Greg even noticed, then silently berated himself for giving the playboy credit for that much sensitivity. Greg was a good friend and a fantastic surgeon, but he was a rotten lover. At least, a rotten lover for Connor. It hurt that he'd walked out.

Connor knew he wanted more than Greg could give him. He wanted commitment, a kind of spiritual connection with the man he would finally decide to settle down with. And Connor did plan on settling down. Casual affairs and buddy fucks left him cold and lonely. He couldn't see spending his life hopping from bed to bed like Greg.

Down the hall, he heard the door to Greg's room slam shut. He let out a deep sigh and sat up. Swinging his legs off the bed, Connor jumped to his feet, careful of his still painfully full erection. He stomped his way to the shower stall and turned the water on full, letting the powerful pulsating showerhead pound over his face and chest before directing the deliciously warm spray over his groin.

He had to admit if nothing else, Greg's

selfishness had its benefits. The man could be a total prick, but he was a caring doctor, generous with his money, despite possessing the customary divine-being complex all surgeons suffered from, especially the really good ones. Greg was an outstanding one and his ego matched his skill.

Grabbing his favorite sponge and a bar of soap off the shelf in the corner of the stall, Connor lathered up and aggressively began to wash the remains of Greg's climax off his body. By the time his frustration and anger faded, his skin was a bright red. He lightened the pressure, moving the wet, slippery sponge lower, trailing the suds slowly down each crease of his groin, deliberately ignoring his leaking cock. After several passes he worked his way around and under his sac, feeling it tighten and pull up at the long awaited attention.

Changing the direction of the showerhead to course over his nipples and tickle down his body, Connor turned the pounding spray to a fine mist to soothe his heated flesh. Relaxing, he closed his eyes and let his usual fantasy lover join him. Usual, since he arrived in Alaska.

From the first night in the isolated settlement five months ago, his wet dreams and fantasies had featured a man Connor knew he had never encountered before. The man's dark, toned body was broad shouldered and well-defined with bulging pecs and a rock hard abdomen. His heavily developed hips met a pair of thick thighs and tapered down to solid calves, all hallmarks of a body builder or a serious runner.

He could never quite see the man's face, but the

veil of black hair swaying past his shoulders was tied off in places with strips of rawhide in the traditional native custom of the northern territory. Whomever his subconscious had created, he was Native American, muscle bound and very, very sensuous.

Sensation and fantasy took over and Connor could actually feel the man's hands as they moved the rough textured sponge over his balls and up his cock. He panted and moaned as the slippery foam battled with the scratch of the porous surface to see which one could dominate his senses. A large, strong hand encased his entire shaft, working the sponge up and down in a firm, leisurely stroke.

Tensing, Connor fell back against the shower wall as the other blunt-fingered hand shoved at his chest, the fingers lingering to pinch and tease one nipple. When the nub was swollen and erect, the hand moved to the other one, twisting and tugging until Connor could barely tolerate the attention.

The stroking of his cock increased in tempo, the wet slide of hand and sponge swirling around the head of his shaft on the up stroke, then sweeping lower to caress his tight sac on the down stroke.

In his mind's eye he could see the bronzed, dripping chest move closer, the unrelenting hands working him faster, the long, sable soft hair swinging down to lightly graze his shoulder, his skin sizzling at every point of contact. The man's sculptured, hairless chest drew near enough that Connor wanted to stick out his tongue and taste the cinnamon colored flesh. He felt his balls draw up closer and his climax churned in the base of his spine, his cock screaming for release from its delicious torture. One more swirling twist over his cock head and Connor bucked up into the vise-like grip, ass clenched tight, cock pulsing out a stream of thick, white cum.

The strength of his orgasm sent a round of white-hot fireworks to explode behind his eyes, making Connor's fantasy lover waver and blur. The smooth skin and rippling muscles transformed into a pelt of thick black fur and the sensual hands shortened into animal paws. A deep guttural growl rolled through Connor's mind and his climax intensified, his balls convulsing until they ached.

Startled by the new twist in his perfect fantasy, Connor lost his footing and slipped, landing hard against the edge of the built-in shelves, knocking a bottle of shampoo to the floor.

"Shit! What the *hell* was that?" He couldn't remember ever being so turned on. Eyes wide and mind reeling, he hurriedly rinsed off the remains of the lather and the copious splatters of cum.

Stepping out of the shower on unsteady legs, Connor toweled off and stumbled out of the bathroom to dress, anxious to keep from seriously examining this sudden attraction to a decidedly primal partner.

***

Chapter Three

Twenty minutes later, comfortably dressed, and hugely sated, with his ego feeling less bruised, Connor ambled down the lodge staircase to the kitchen. He grabbed a cup of coffee from a steaming coffeepot and made his way through the huge, comfortable sitting room to the connecting hallway leading from the lodge into the clinic.

Greg's money had been freely spent remodeling the old, log lodge. The front half had been transformed into a modern day clinic and surgery, while the back was now a cozy, rustic lodge with a charming center living room, a massive fireplace, a huge dining room and a spacious kitchen. The second story boasted enough bedrooms to house up to five staff members comfortably. The bedrooms were warm and spacious. Each had its own well-appointed, private bath.

An enthusiastic outdoorsman with a lifetime of privilege and riches, the hedonistic, spoiled man brought with him as many of life's little luxuries as his family's fortune and a bush plane could ship into a remote Alaskan settlement.

The lodge was luxurious in a rustic, charming way, but Connor still never understood why Greg stayed. Living in this remote land far from the spotlight really deviated from the playboy persona Greg presented to the world.

Connor suspected something big had happened to make him isolate himself up here. He also suspected

Greg would never feel comfortable telling him about it since he knew in his heart that they were just physical lovers, not soul mates. All Connor knew for certain about the place was that Greg had established the clinic after visiting the region on a hunting trip three years ago and had never left.

Sipping from the cup of rich, gourmet coffee in his hand, Connor reminded himself he really shouldn't complain. Everyone in the little town had benefited from Greg's self-indulgence, especially his medical staff and the local workers that helped keep the clinic running. Life in the remote town of Nekenano was better since Greg Pierce arrived.

When his contract expired in a month, Connor didn't know if he'd stay. Connor wasn't sure he and Greg would stay together as lovers. He never liked being alone. The people here weren't prejudiced about gays, but there just didn't seem to be anyone else besides Greg and himself. He didn't think he could stay in a relationship just for the sex, but he didn't want to stay someplace where there was no hope of having an intimate relationship, either.

Sighing, Connor downed another satisfying gulp of the hot liquid and pushed open the heavy door to the clinic waiting room. The large room was lined with firm, comfortable chairs and several small couches. There were table lamps and floor lamps in unobtrusive places, throwing a soft glow into the corners of the functional but stylish room.

At the far end, an open area framed by half walls defined the nurses' station and office area. Over the rough-hewn logs and the thick white chinking, colorful posters of every imaginable subject lined the walls, making an interesting, if eclectic, wallpaper. A raised hearth held a cheery fire behind a child-safe, iron gate.

The first person Connor saw was Greg leaning against the countertop, gray canvas Dockers neatly pressed and perfectly coordinated with a muted charcoal sweater that brought out the silver flecks in his hazel eyes, sipping coffee. His dark curls were casually tousled, still rakishly damp from the shower. Dr. Greg Pierce was definitely out to impress.

Connor almost considered dragging the man back to bed, but the sight of the offending green scarf around Greg's neck immediately changed his mind. Instead, he ran a hand through his own wet hair, flopped his overly long bangs out of his eyes and tried to smooth the wrinkles from his favorite blue flannel shirt. Dismissing Greg with a curt nod, he turned to greet the other man in the room.

"Morning, Mitch." Connor raised his mug, gesturing toward the kitchen at the back of the house with it. "There's fresh coffee in the kitchen."

"Thanks, Doc. I already had some. That's the second pot. Dark drank the first one."

Handsome in a rugged, weathered way, with long black hair and sharp clean features, Mitch Red Elk was one of two Native American guides employed by the clinic. The other guide, Dark Eaglehawk, was usually with Mitch in the mornings. Connor assumed the older guide was greeting the new doctor at the airstrip.

The guides' primary function was to help out when the doctors had to go on house calls or needed

20

transport to remote hunting sites for emergencies. The two men spent a good deal of their time doing small projects around the lodge and running errands for the doctors and staff.

"Figures. You and Dark are always the first ones up. You two never seem to sleep." Connor arched his back until he heard the satisfying pop of vertebra snapping. "I don't know how you do it."

Mitch smiled, a mischievous sparkle lighting up his black eyes. "We sleep." His usual dry humor surfaced. "We just do it alone. Makes it a lot easier to get up on time."

Feeling the rush of blood to his cheeks, Connor grunted and dipped his head, pretending to sip coffee until the silence became uncomfortable. He looked up to see the corner of Greg's lips twitch with the obvious effort to hold back a smile. The hurt from earlier flared up from the dying embers of what fast was becoming the remains of their relationship.

Staring directly into Greg's laughing eyes Connor quietly said, "That's sound advice, Mitch. I think I'll be taking it from here on out." The spark of amusement dimmed in Greg's eyes, leaving him open mouthed and speechless.

Connor turned his back and walked away to stare out the large glass windows lining the front of the waiting room. Walking past the tall, broad-shouldered guide, Connor was relieved to see Mitch's usual neutral expression back in place. It was hard enough to deal with Greg mocking him this early in the morning, he didn't need someone else joining in.

The slight shuffle of feet on the thick carpet told

him one of the two men had followed him. He was pretty sure whom it was when familiar, long-fingered hands gripped his shoulders and began to massage the tense muscles in a decidedly seductive manner.

"Come on, Connor, don't be like that." Greg lowered his voice to a husky whisper that sent shivers down Connor's spine. "I *really* needed to leave." His voice took on a tone of pleading sincerity. "The plane's already landed. Dark will be here with the new man any minute."

A light cough reminded them Mitch was still in the room. Connor leaned slightly away from Greg's restraining hands. Greg didn't seem to register the sound, ignoring it, just like he usually ignored most of what Mitch said and did.

A discreet murmur floated by them as Mitch headed out of the room. "Guess I'll get that extra cup of coffee, after all." The door between the clinic and the lodge clicked firmly shut.

Greg stepped close to Connor's back and blew in his ear between words. "You know how much I like making love to you, lover." He dipped the tip of his tongue into the outer shell to moisten it, then breathed heavily over it, making Connor shiver as warm air struck wet skin. "Sucking you off," he whispered, then mouthed the small ear lobe, "rubbing our swollen cocks together," then nibbled on it, "making you cum all over me."

The heat of Greg's body radiated through both layers of clothing and scalded Connor's back. The fresh scent of soap and expensive cologne filled his head, bringing back memories of happier, more content times.

Connor sighed and let his body relax into the familiar warmth of Greg's taller, broader frame. The nibbling changed to light kissing of the sensitive skin behind his ear, a weak spot of his, and a pair of arms moved down to wind possessively around his waist.

Greg turned Connor in his arms and began raining soft, chaste kisses over his face. "I'm sorry. I don't want to fight, okay?"

Before Connor could answer, Greg kissed him hard and deep, exploring every inch of his mouth and sucking on his tongue until his cock started to harden in his jeans. This reminded Connor of why he got involved with the man in the first place. Six foot two inches of hot, liquid sex attached to a mouth like a vacuum. He felt his emotions tumble from angry to merely disgruntled to receptive and forgiving in the time it took Greg to complete his thorough examination of his open, willing mouth.

When Connor moaned, Greg broke away, then kissed his way around the line of Connor's jaw and started down his neck.

Connor let himself sink into the sensations, enjoying the moment despite the circumstances. Making out in the clinic, in front of a large glass wall, wasn't the most professional thing they could be doing. The entire town knew they were lovers, but the moments when Greg was demonstrative in public were rare. Connor was going to savor this one for as long as he could. Besides, maybe make-up sex would be more satisfying.

Greg kissed him again, hard and demanding. Connor gave in to the hot, urgent embrace and

23

his imagination took over. Suddenly, he was wrapped in the arms of a larger lover, being devoured by an unfamiliar set of full insistent lips. His hips were crushed against a hard groin. He could feel a thick shaft grinding into his own, pulsing with excitement and need. His sexual desire soared and he felt like he was going to explode when suddenly, the same deep animal growl he'd heard in the shower, rumbled in his ear.

Startled, he jumped back out of Greg's arms and stood staring at him, panting, wide-eyed and shaking at the intensity of the fantasy.

Greg stared back at him, an injured, confused expression on his flushed face. He licked at his lips, arms held open and empty. "What? I said I was sorry! What's wrong with you?"

He stepped closer, eyes searching Connor's face, taking in his trembling and confused gaze. The injured look disappeared from Greg's face to be replaced with genuine concern. He bent down to look his lover directly in the eyes and took hold of his upper arms to steady him. "Are you okay, Connor?"

"Yeah, yeah, I'm fine. I just had a little…" He grabbed hold of Greg's arms and pulled in several deep breaths. When he felt the blood pounding through his head subside to a dull roar, he shook his head. "I don't know what it was."

He wasn't about to reveal what had really happened. He doubted Greg would appreciate having been replaced in Connor's thoughts while kissing him. "Must have been lack of air. I just got dizzy. I'm fine now, really."

Spots danced in front of his eyes and he

stumbled a little as Greg started to guide him to a chair. Suddenly another pair of hands, stronger and wider, wrapped around his waist and guided him down onto the seat. Mitch had reappeared so quickly even the lodge door hadn't clicked shut before he was at Connor's side.

"Keep your head down." Mitch squatted in front of Connor looking up at him, calming black eyes locked onto frightened green. "You'll be fine, trust me. It'll pass."

The rich, deep tone of Mitch's low voice was filled with confidence, and for no good reason, it made Connor feel better. Leaning back in the chair, he nodded his thanks. Another shiver shook his entire body. A warm blanket engulfed him as Greg crouched down beside Mitch to pull it tightly around him. A worried frown on his lips, Greg rested his hands on Connor's knee.

"Are you sure you're all right? I mean, you're not sick, are you?" His hand flew to Connor's forehead to feel for a fever. Connor reached up and gently pulled it away.

"I'm fine. I just got lightheaded. *Someone*," he glared at Greg, "woke me up too early and I haven't had enough coffee yet. I'm fine."

"You're sure? Because I can meet with this new guy alone, Connor, really. You two can touch base later. Go lay down for awhile."

His hand reached for Connor's head again, but the other man intercepted it and pushed it away. "Stop playing doctor, Greg, *I'm fine*."

Mischief in his eyes, Mitch softly chuckled. "If

you ask me, 'playing doctor' is what caused this, Doc."

"Very funny." Connor's mouth twisted in a grimace. He sounded tired, but tolerant.

Greg nudged Mitch from out in front of Connor and pulled the blanket up over the smaller man's shoulders and sniffed. "I don't remember either of us asking, Mitch," he frowned, darting a glare at the man. "Shouldn't you go help Dark bring back the new guy and check on the supplies coming in?"

"Don't need to." Mitch smirked.

Greg shoved Mitch's greater bulk to one side. Mitch quietly followed Greg's every move.

Without turning to look at the guide, Greg huffed and fussed, wordlessly tipping up Connor's head into the light to check his pupils. "Well, *maybe*, you should do it anyway."

Rising to his feet in one fluid movement, Mitch patted Connor's shoulder and walked towards the front door to the clinic. "Don't have to, they're already here."

Outside, the temperature hovered just above zero, creating a ring of frost around the entire plate glass window of the clinic, challenging even the thermal-paned, double-layered glass the lodge boasted. It was still pitch black and snowing lightly, masking anything more than four feet from the window. Soon the sound of a snow machine rattled through the glass, drowning out the noise of the old pickup truck that followed it to the curb out front.

They all watched as two people tumbled out of the truck cab and hastened toward the clinic. Two more people from the snow machine followed at a more leisurely pace. All were bundled in arctic clothing, faces and genders lost in the thick layers and folds of fabric and fur.

Mitch opened the door and shooed them in. He nodded a greeting at a tall, lanky man wearing a baseball cap and chewing on an unlit, mangled cigar. He wordlessly looked over the next two people in the group then turned to the last man through the door. Small but wiry, the 50-ish looking man with short, graying black hair and a weathered face was the clinic's second guide.

"You made it back. Doc Pierce was beginning to worry about you." Mitch clapped the man on the shoulder.

The man grunted. "And you should not tell lies. Makes your hair fall out."

The newly arrived guide went by the simple name of Dark, claiming his mother named him after a medicine woman foretold his future shortly after his birth. Oddly, Connor could never find anything even remotely dark about the man. He was quiet, but cheerful, friendly and comforting to be around. Connor enjoyed his company and listened endlessly to the stories and legends the older man told him.

Seeing Connor hunched on the chair, Greg solicitously at his side, Dark asked, "What's wrong with the young one?" His face knotted up into a concerned frown.

Mitch cocked his head, and shrugged one shoulder, lowering his voice so Dark was the only one within hearing. "Vision, I think. Scared him."

Sighing heavily, Dark shook his head, eyes still watching the pair. "His spirits are strong, but the

27

ancient ones pull at him, and I do not think he is ready."
His face darkened and the heavy lines around his
mouth grew more pronounced. "Accepting the path the
spirits have chosen for him will be difficult, especially
for a man of modern white man's medicine."

"He is a two spirit. He was marked early in life.
The moon has claimed him as her own. There is no
going back." Mitch drew in a deep breath and nodded,
seeming to evaluate Connor, then adding, "He is strong
enough." He smiled and clapped Dark on the back,
shaking him. "And you will be with him. Tell him the
stories of the old ones again. Help him understand.
Before it grows too late."

The older guide silently nodded and walked
over to stand unobtrusively at Connor's side. By an
unspoken pact, Dark had been appointed Connor's
guide, while Mitch always paired with Greg. After just
a few weeks, Connor had quickly looked to Dark as a
sort of father figure.

Three years later, Greg still didn't seem to think
about Mitch at all. He just accepted the man's presence
at his side and had grown to expect it. Neither guide
complained.

Mitch disappeared in the direction of the kitchen
and returned with four steaming mugs of coffee. He
drank it black and so did anyone he got coffee for,
whether they liked it that way or not.

The three remaining new additions to the room
stood huddled in front of the fireplace, slowly stripping
away layer after layer of clothing. John Trumble, the
bush pilot who serviced the area with regular flights in
and out of Nekenano for supplies, transportation and

28

the occasional emergency, finished first.

Turning his baseball hat around backwards, Trumble pulled the well-chewed cigar from his mouth, using it to punctuate his sentences as he talked. He ambled over to the men by Connor's chair, taking a cup from Mitch as he walked by.

"Hey there, Docs. What's cooking?" One look at Connor's flushed face and Greg's pinched expression and Trumble asked, "Something wrong? Is the kid sick?" His eyes darted up to question Dark, then bounced down to look at Greg. "Brought that replacement for Tom just in time then, huh?"

Greg glanced up at the man. "Hi, John. Welcome back." Connor watched as Greg shot a quick look at the two people by the fire, obviously curious about them. Nothing could be distinguished except several figures backlit in bright yellow flames. Greg's gaze darted back down to Connor. "I don't think he's sick, just tired."

"I'm not sick, or tired, or anything." Connor shrugged off the blanket and clambered up to his feet. "I'm fine."

He tucked in his rumpled shirt and smoothed out the wrinkles, trying to get back to normal. He still felt vaguely disconnected to the present moment, but he was no longer dizzy or frightened. "I wish everyone would just let it go."

Greg followed his lover to his feet. "You're sure? I mean, you look better. Your pupils look normal, but you're still a little flushed."

Connor could feel Greg's sharp, clinical eyes noting everything about him. He pursed his lips and gave Greg a sour glare. "I think the flush can be explained, Greg." He glanced meaningfully at the other man's still half-hard cock clearly outlined by his snug pants.

Following Connor's gaze, Greg glanced down at his groin and smiled. "Well," he cleared his throat, "okay. That seems logical." The grin broke free. "Acceptable even."

Snorting lightly, Connor gave him a small, wry smile back. "Really, I'm fine. Stop worrying." Connor retreated away from the tight circle of worried expressions and moved to where Mitch stood halfway between the two clusters of people, bridging the gap between the old and the new. He stole a cup of coffee from the guide and sipped it, letting the caffeine revive his flagging energy.

Satisfied Connor was fully recovered, Greg turned to take in the new arrivals. One of the genderless forms had turned into a woman. Gabe Walker down at the garage had warned them his sister was coming to visit soon. She must have been a part of the transport John had brought into town.

She had mousy brown hair worn in a short bob cut and pale, plain features. Of average height and build, she was unremarkable except for the cool, sharp blue eyes that screamed of intelligence. The slight twist to her thin lips spoke of a demanding nature. Even now her head was held high and her pointy chin extended farther than her nearly absent breasts did. She ignored Greg's stare as she finger-combed her hair, then turned away to warm her hands by the fire.

Gabe had described his sister as part dragon and

part mule. Watching her, Greg had to agree with the assessment.

Dismissing her as Gabe's problem, Greg turned his attention to the last newcomer just as the man pulled off his hat and earmuffs. Greg held his breath and moved closer to get a better look.

The man was gorgeous. Thick, honey blond hair framed a flawless complexion. His high-boned cheeks were separated by a long, sculptured nose and topped by a pair of intense gray eyes. His dark pink lips were full and he seemed to have a habit of licking them frequently, keeping them moist and shiny. The thick, bulky parka slid from his shoulders revealing a trim, athletic body. Greg nearly gasped out loud when the man turned and caught his eye, giving him a warm smile that was part sensual leer.

Connor stood watching the entire scene from a corner of the room while John chatted with Dark and Mitch.

Still feeling disconnected from everyone in the room, he was surprised to find his feelings were only slightly bruised by Greg's blatant interest in the other man. A small, elusive ache blossomed under his breastbone.

He realized things were slowly crawling to an end between Greg and himself. They weren't right as a couple for anything other than hot sex. But Greg would always be his friend.

And now, Greg was on the prowl. Connor just wished he wasn't stuck here watching it.

Pushing off the wall he was leaning against, he started for the door to the lodge, deciding to excuse himself to go lie down after all. He'd force himself to be pleasant to the perfect Dr. Ashton Webb after he'd had a little time to get some distance from the situation. His flight from the room was interrupted when the local deputy, Joss Crow, jogged through the door from the street, breathless and red-faced.

"Hey, Doc Pierce!" Joss waited until Greg flung a half interested look his way. "Abe just got a call over the radio. Justin Loken's new bride, the little sixteen-year-old girl that's expecting?"

That got everyone's attention. Greg turned to face Joss, focusing on his every word. "She's due in two weeks. Justin's supposed to bring her into town in a few days so she can be here to deliver."

Joss threw his hands in the air. "Well, she ain't gonna make it. He radioed to say she went into labor last night and things are going pretty hard on her. He wants to know if one of you docs can come out to their place, pronto."

Dark broke away from his conversation with the pilot. "That's at least four hours away from here." He looked at Mitch and they exchanged an anxious glance. "Up north in Raven Gully."

Pulling a pre-packed rucksack from a wide, built-in closet by the nurses' station, Greg began checking it for supplies. "You know *exactly* where it is?"

Mitch joined him and in seconds they had the needed equipment and supplies waiting at their feet. Dark nodded, but frowned. "Yes, but it's not easy to get to."

Greg looked uncertainly from Connor to the new man.

Putting down his coffee cup, Connor stepped in and made the decision easy for him. He wanted to get away for awhile anyway.

"I'll go. You get Dr. Webb settled in." Unable to keep an edge of bitterness out of his voice, he added, "Acquaint him with all of the personal amenities the clinic has to offer." He pushed past Greg and picked his fur-lined parka off the wall hook behind the counter.

Dark grabbed the two packs and headed out, calling over his shoulder to Connor, "I'll get the machine loaded up, Doc."

"Connor, wait." Greg blocked Connor's way. Grabbing Connor's arms, he lowered his voice to a pleading whisper. "Don't be like that. I'm just doing my job here. Making the guy feel welcome." He glanced up at Webb's still leering smile and colored slightly. "You don't have anything to worry about. Honestly. I'll still be here when you get back."

Connor slowly pulled out of Greg's restraining hands and stepped back. "I'm not worried, Greg. The question is, will I want to stay here once I come back?" He patted Greg's chest and fingered the soft cashmere scarf thrown casually around his neck. A sudden impulse struck him and he pulled the scarf off Greg and wound it around his own neck.

Greg's fingers followed the scarf, involuntarily twitching, grabbing at thin air. "Hey! What are you doing?"

Connor wrapped the scarf tighter and tucked the ends into his coat. "Insurance. It'll give you a reason to look forward to my coming back." The corners of his tight smile turned down a fraction. "And it might be the only thing I get out of this relationship."

He quickly shouldered the remaining pack, then headed outside as Dark started up the snow machine at the curb.

Greg followed him to the door and watched him depart. He returned the small, lackluster wave Connor gave him just as they pulled away from the curb. Sighing, he turned back to see a room full of expectant stares. Greg focused on the new man and walked towards him, hand extended in welcome and a smile on his charming face.

"Dr. Webb? I'm Greg Pierce. Welcome to Nekenano and the Pierce Clinic." Greg's bright, welcoming smile dimmed a little as the man's expression became confused.

The man reached out and warmly shook Greg's hand, but his eyes darted to the woman still standing at the fireplace. "I think there's been some kind of mistake."

"Mistake?" Greg's smile froze and slipped a little. He swept his eyes from Webb to the woman and back. Behind him, Trumble chuckled, then coughed into his shirtsleeve. "What kind of mistake?"

The man's smile stayed warm and seductively inviting, but Greg's blood ran cold at his words. "My name's Roger Seaton. I'm John's new co-pilot. I'll be visiting on the monthly supply runs, but I'm not your new doc." The man pointed at the dragon lady patiently waiting, arms crossed and expression unimpressed. "She is."

Huffing out a mirthless chuckle, Greg turned and shook the woman's hand, speechless for the first time in years.

The woman smiled and looked him over from head to toe. "When the interviewer happened to asked if I was gay, I thought you wanted to know if I was a happy person." She smirked and twirled a strand of her hair. "So, of course, I said yes."

The strangled coughing from the other end of the room increased. Greg grimaced and shot Mitch and John a condemning glare, then smiled hollowly at Webb. "Of course. And I'm happy you're happy. We're all just one big happy family here. Mitch'll show where you can put your things."

Webb returned his false smile and Greg walked away as the guide motioned for her to follow him into the lodge.

Looking out the window at Connor's disappearing tracks in the snow, Greg paled and wondered just how badly Connor was going to make him pay before he got back in the young man's good graces. He somehow felt his beloved scarf was going to be a small sacrifice before this was all over.

***

Chapter Four

One of the reasons Connor became a doctor was because of how impressed he was with Mother Nature, her restorative powers and the awesome wonder of the body's ability to heal and adapt to change. How much the human body and spirit could withstand and still remain whole constantly amazed him. It fueled his calling to medicine with the burning desire to understand its timeless secrets.

Now he stood in an isolated, snow-blanketed valley, thousands of miles from everything he knew and hundreds of miles from any sizable gathering of people.

Outside the rough-hewn log cabin, perched on a frozen knoll of ice between smatterings of scrub trees, Connor carefully drew in a breath of freezing arctic air and watched the frost drift by as he exhaled. The sting of the cold left his lungs tingling with a light burning sensation and his nostril hairs immediately froze together. Scrunching his nose to free the hairs, he switched to open-mouth breathing, forcing the air to come in through the layers of fabric wrapped around his mouth and most of his face.

The winds kicked up and he pulled his protective goggles into place from the top of his head. After spending five difficult hours helping the young couple in the drafty, small cabin behind him, he had delivered their first son into the world. Tired and cold, he was ready to head back to town and the comfort and warmth of his own downy, blanket-heaped bed.

Out There in the Night

The birth had been difficult under the primitive conditions, and the mother was small boned, but it had been exhilarating at the same time. He loved helping to bring a baby into the world. It always made him feel content and slightly like the right hand of God.

The snap and crunch of a rigid, uncooperative door being closed behind him alerted Connor that Dark had finally followed him outside. He turned and gave the older man a thumbs-up to indicate he was ready to leave. The guide returned his gesture with a sharp, abbreviated jerk of his head and slowly trudged over to their snow machine, his hooded, dark eyes restlessly searching the surrounding tundra in anxious, irregular waves.

Made nervous by the guide's unusual actions, Connor's gaze flashed involuntarily over the same shadowed wasteland, seeing nothing that hadn't been there when they arrived. A sudden feeling of anxiety tingled at the back of his neck, deep under his cashmere trophy. Everything about Dark on this trip, from his silent responses, to his tense, abrupt body language, was making Connor jumpy and on edge. Connor hunched his shoulders and buried his chin in the folds of his fur-lined parka.

During his months in Nekenano, Connor had been spellbound by the local stories Dark told of the original Indian settlement and the ancient Dena'ina warrior tribe who made the desolate, frozen wasteland their home for hundreds of years. Drawn to the legends and myths, his curiosity had exploded with a need to explore the mysterious, ancient culture.

Right now, standing in the growing twilight,

wind howling eerily and biting at his cheeks, he wasn't so eager to explore anything, but the warm corners of the old lodge back in town.

Dark started the snow machine; making it howl out a loud, low rumble of manmade power. He gunned the engine twice, dark eyes still searching the twilight-shrouded trees surrounding the tiny dwelling.

Both Connor and Dark started when the noise of the snow machine was answered by a howl in the distance. An eerie, spine tingling sound that echoed off the hills and sent a shiver all the way through to the pit of Connor's stomach. Another, much closer howl sounded to their left. He cast an anxious glance at Dark.

"What was that? Wolves?"

Without taking his gaze from the darkening hillside, the guide slowly nodded, then impatiently jerked his head to one side to indicate the seat waiting behind him.

"Come on, son. The spiritwalkers seem to be in a hurry. Your two-spirits must be very powerful for them to want you so badly."

"Huh?" A mournful howl sounded closer to their position.

Confused, but more anxious than curious, Connor didn't wait for an answer. He lost no time in mounting the snow machine, lacing his arms securely around the other man's waist. He was as adventurous as the next man, but not foolish enough to want to meet a pack of wolves on the hunt, even with the rifle he knew Dark carried.

As soon as he was on board, Dark gunned the machine again and headed out toward home, wasting no time on leisurely building up speed.

The trees blurred past Connor as they turned in front of the cabin. He caught sight of Justin's face in the open doorway and his heart skipped a beat. A cold sweat broke out over his entire body. Connor increased his hold on Dark, continuing to stare at the cabin as the sight of Justin disappeared into the twilight. Berating himself over a burst of irrational fear, he told himself it was just a trick of the fading arctic light. Five miles later, he still couldn't rid himself of the memory of Justin's eyes as they turned to glowing yellow.

Connor was still thinking about it when Dark unexpectedly shifted forward on the seat, turning to yell a warning that was lost to Connor, whipped away by the battering winds. The haunting vision of bright yellow eyes transferred from inside Connor's head to in front of his face, as a heavy weight knocked into his face and chest. He was thrown from the snow machine, the back of his head striking the concrete-hard ice as he landed.

The fading evening light dimmed and blurred around Connor, the harsh coughing sound of the snow machine unnaturally far away, then eerily gone altogether. Connor felt a seeping, wet warmth on his face and down the back of his neck, then everything slipped away, escorted by a blinding pain that shot through the back of his head.

***

It was the scent that drew him. The unmistakably masculine odor of sweat and testosterone mixed with a large measure of fear. The smell of fear attracted him first, but the rich, bittersweet odor of the man's sweat was what kept him on the human's trail. The sharp tang made his sensitive nostrils flare and his muzzle whiskers prickle erect with excitement. His groin reacted with the same response, growing heavy and engorged, the glistening tip emerging from its protective sleeve of stiff bristles and tough flesh.

His massive paws pounded over the deep snow, navigating the icy ground with the graceful agility of a wild animal, narrowing the distance between predator and prey with rapid determination. He slowed when he came within visual range of his prey, boldly standing illuminated in the blue-white moonlight, his dark coat standing out starkly against the surrounding snow-covered land.

The scent of blood was also thick in the air, swirling and dipping through the night, pushed along by the howling winds, each gust calling him to this prey, to this spot. It had been one hundred years since he had physically been in this place, though he visited it often in his dreams. This was the place of the spiritwalkers. He knew that being called to return in real, physical form meant his life was about to change again.

He prowled over an outcropping of rocks, watching the small, still figure in the distance, scenting the air, making sure this was the one meant for him and him alone. A hard gust of wind, full of the human's smell, assaulted his nose when he took too long staring. Both his senses and his cock felt a fresh surge of electric-filled anticipation and lust. He began to pant and prance, anxious for more contact, more stimulation, more satisfaction.

Working his way around the perimeter where the human lay, he marked his territory every few yards. Rubbing his hindquarters over the ground or a tree stimulated the glands located at the base of his tail to leak a scented oil, ensuring his prize was clearly marked as his to claim. The remainder of his pack was several miles behind, keeping a respectful distance, mindful of the fierce alpha male's intent in this particular hunt.

The annoying machine the humans had been riding on was finally silent and still, several yards away from the human male sprawled on the hard, icy ground. Its rough howling voice no longer echoed off the hillsides, shattering the peace of the night. Beside it, another human lay in a tangled heap, limbs askew at odd angles.

A young, yellow-eyed wolf paced on the outer perimeter of a small circle he had just marked. The young one whined and groveled, showing the proper submissive posturing to the dark one's alpha status. Briefly acknowledged by a deep growl and a nip from the black wolf, it backed away into the darkness to set up a sentry position on the top of the nearest knoll. The alpha ignored it as the spiritwalkers came to him, dancing on the winds, pleased he had arrived.

Brazen as only a top-of-the-food-chain predator could be, he moved directly to the small human's side. Sniffing the puddle of congealed blood pooled under the man's head, he nuzzled aside the layers of fabric protecting the human's face from the wind, nostrils filled with the unwelcome scent of another male that

41

was neither this human's nor his companion's. Even the delicious odor of the yellow-haired one's blood caked over a deep, jagged wound on his forehead couldn't dispel the sexual mating challenge the unwelcome scent brought out in him.

Incensed by the odor on what he claimed as his own, he tore viciously at the soft strip of cloth around the small male's neck until it came free, heedless of the bright red claw and teeth marks he left behind. Seizing the freed scarf between his forepaws and powerful jaws, he shredded it until nothing more than tiny squares of green tatters remained to be whisked away by the increasing arctic winds.

Finally satisfied, he sniffed the air to be sure all traces of the rival had been eradicated. Once again his sensitive nostrils were overwhelmed by the rich, heady scent of his original prey.

The natural scent of the man's body, mixed with the bitter tang of blood and the lingering smell of panic and fear, sent a shiver of primal lust through his sinewy, powerhouse frame. His nostrils flared, their sensitive nerve endings burning. He licked at the exposed skin of the man's hairless face, washing away the blood from his chin.

Tantalized by the flavor and richness of the blood, he hunched down over the limp body, covering it protectively with his own, boldly lapping at the man's parted lips. He tasted the slight moisture left behind with each warm puff of breath the man exhaled, the provocative flavor renewed time and time again. His long tongue slithered against the roof of the man's mouth, caressing and twirling against the sensitive tissue until the unconscious man groaned a low, pained, but responsive sound.

Encouraged, his rusty orange eyes glowed brighter. He settled the bulk of his fur-covered torso down onto the man, keeping part of his weight on his strong front legs. Thrilled by the way his lean hips fitted perfectly between the man's outstretched legs, he nestled his cock, protective bristle sheath already retracted several inches in excitement, over the growing bulge of the man's groin. He snarled and whined, instinctively humping his hindquarters against the slender form pinned underneath. The man moaned and moved restlessly at the intimate contact. He caught the faint whiff of hormones released into the air.

Lust-filled excitement seized him and his exploration of the man's parted mouth became frenzied along with the rhythmic, fluid movements of his hips. Long strokes of his meaty tongue slid down the man's throat and his own thin, furred lips raked short bristles over the man's smooth, warm lips. He snarled and pawed at the clothing presenting a barrier between himself and his intended mate, tearing through thick protective layers with stunning ease.

Just before he exposed sensitive skin to the effects of the biting arctic wind and cold, a harsh warning yip and growl drew his attention.

On the fringe of the few scraggily trees surrounding the gully stood an old gray wolf. The gray wolf dipped his head and lowered his front half in the traditional signal of submission, but he continued to growl and yip, then howl, never taking his gaze from the larger wolf.

The eerie, singsong rhythm of the howling seemed to calm the alpha leader. He slowly raised his body and gave the parted, now mumbling mouth one last long, thorough lap.

Rising to his hind feet to stand well over six-foot tall, the black wolf now resembled a man in an ancient Indian headdress and fur robe more than a wild beast. His rust colored eyes reflected a keen intelligence, and for the first time, the two silver bands adorned with several feathers braided into the fur at the side of his head were noticeable. Barrel-chested with rippling, corded muscles and raw, primal energy exuding from every fiber of his being, he made an obvious effort to reign in his lust. Giving a disgruntled snarl, he nodded to the old gray, who slowly let his howl fade away on the increasing winds.

The black wolf walked to the body of the second man and stared down into the guide's half-hooded, glazed-over eyes, and listened to the man's stuttering heartbeat. Aware the old Indian would probably not survive his many injuries, he offered up a short howl to lament his coming journey to the spirit world. A brief flicker of stunned recognition in the guide's eyes was acknowledged with a tilt of his head before he turned away to retrieve his mate, the ultimate goal of this particular hunt.

The black wolf, now fully transformed into the more powerful form of werewolf, carefully scooped up Dr. Connor Jacy from the frozen ground and buried the man's exposed face and chest against his own thick outer coat of fur.

Face thrown back into the blinding, snow-filled

wind, the black werewolf sniffed the air, his lips curled back in a parody of a human smile. His pack was near, his mate was secured, no other unfriendly humans save the dying guide were in his territory and the faint scent of his arousal still lingered on the night air. It was as the spiritwalkers had said. It was a night of many blessings.

Satisfied, he pointed his muzzle where he knew the moon shone in the cloud-shrouded sky and let loose with a triumphant howl of such magnitude it shook a layer of snow from the surrounding tree limbs.

The howl echoed off the gully walls and Connor responded, moving restlessly against the thick chest. Pain-dulled eyes fluttered open and Connor blearily looked up into the rusty orange stare of a wild beast. His eyes widened in disbelief, blinking rapidly to dispel what had to be another trick of the fading light and too many recently told native legends. Pain made the battle to focus too difficult to tolerate and his eyes flickered closed again. Giving in to the pull of unconsciousness, he burrowed deeper into the warmth of the coarse fur and protective body heat.

The werewolf growled deep in his chest at the unexpected sight of his mate's crystal green eyes. This mate was as precious as the spiritwalkers had foretold. Hair like sunlight and eyes the color of the springtime grasses, this two-spirit would bring the daylight with him into the werewolf's night-shrouded world.

His lonely, century-long wait for a life mate at an end, Adam Lowell pressed his heart's one true desire closer and leapt out of the clearing, flanked at a respectful distance by the gray wolf.

***

The huge black skinwalker entered the small, one room cabin his human half called home, still cradling Connor's lax body tightly to his chest. The howl of the gathering winds rattled the glass panes in the single cabin window and snow piled over the threshold before he could kick the door closed with a massive paw. Passing a large stone hearth filled with the glowing embers of a recent fire, he loped to a rectangular wooden table and gently deposited Connor on it, cautiously supporting the man's injured head.

Satisfied Connor was going to remain unconscious and immobile, Adam closed his eyes and transformed into his human form. Nude, he went to the fireplace and added several logs to the embers, fanning them back to life. When he had a healthy roar and crackle in the hearth, he hung up a water-filled kettle to heat. The smell of birch hung in the air as thin tendrils of smoke escaped the chimney and drifted into the room. The chilly temperature rose quickly in the small, sturdy room.

Adam drew a large Bowie knife from a sheath on the stone mantle and began cutting off Connor's clothing, piece by piece. He saved his parka, boots and thick socks, but every other item was sliced and discarded. Stained with blood and smelling faintly like the destroyed scarf, they were thrown into the fire to burn.

Once Connor was completely naked, Adam ran his callused hands gently over every square inch of the pale smooth body, searching for broken bones and sensing for damaged tissues. Finding several bruises and abrasions on Connor's left side, Adam retrieved the warm water from the fire and began cleaning the shallow wounds. Just as he finished, the front door opened and the old gray wolf sauntered in, closing the door behind him.

Adam gave him a quick glance of acknowledgment. The wolf shifted and took human form, transforming into an older version of Adam, tall, broad, and dark. He carried the mark of many seasons in the weathered wrinkles of his face and the gnarled curl of his hands, but his eyes were clear and full of wisdom. Around his neck he wore the trappings of their native culture, amulets and charms, showing him to be a powerful medicine man. Out of respect for the alpha male's new mate, the old shaman took a robe from a hook by the door and slipped into it, then joined Adam at the table.

"Are his wounds of importance?" The older man's voice was deep and rough, worn with passage of the many years that had passed before he had been blessed by the spirits with the gift of being a skinwalker.

Adam shook his head, never taking his gaze from Connor, fingers cautiously kneading through his mass of bloodstained, golden hair.

"His body is whole, Dyami, but his head has been split on both back and front. The wounds are slight, but the damage may be grave."

The old man peeled back Connor's eyelids to stare into his dull green eyes, grunted, and then pulled an elk skin pouch from under the table. He wordlessly began removing items from the bag and arranging them close at hand.

Chanting softly, the old shaman set four small pots, each filled with a chunk of something from the pouch, in the corners of the room and lit them with a strip of kindling from the fire. A dense, sweet odor drifted into the air.

The room continued to grow warmer and the increase in temperature pulled the chill from Connor's body, warming his flesh and allowing his blood to flow more freely. A small puddle of blood pooled under his head from the hidden wound and a thin trickle oozed from the wound on his forehead.

Adam sponged the blood from the front of Connor's face and gently inspected the deep laceration on the left side, just below his hairline. The gaping wound was jagged, with several short lacerations fanning out around it. Once wiped free of blood, Adam pressed a clean cloth to it and gestured for the other man to help turn Connor over.

Carefully placing the smaller man onto his chest, Adam tenderly turned Connor's head the left to put pressure on the facial wound and still allow him to breathe.

Once carefully positioned, Adam began sponging the dried blood from his hair and scalp, working his way to the still oozing wound where Connor's head had struck the rock-hard ice. Kneading the flesh, Adam found a four-inch diameter pocket of swelling with a rough-edged opening where Connor's skin had split on impact.

Mouth set in a grim line, Adam glanced up at

the holy man, pushing aside the matted thatch of Connor's hair to show him the wound.

Adam spoke in a low, non-condemning tone, a note of unhappy resignation in his words. "The young one who prevented them from leaving the gully was a bit too energetic in his efforts. My mate has suffered more than expected."

The shaman's soft chanting had continued the entire time Adam and he had been working, but now he paused. "But not more than the spirits wished. All has purpose, Adam. Trust this does, too. Your mate is strong. During this time of healing, you will care for him and grow to know him. Use the time wisely."

The eerie, singsong chant began again, increasing in volume, the tone urgent and commanding, calling to the spirit world. Soon the shadows of the room inched closer, moving in time to the chanting, long tendrils of black weaving their way into the room and around the three men.

Thin wisps of smoke-laced shadows guided Adam's hand as he meticulously stitched the small wound closed with catgut and needle. More wisps swirled around Connor, sending whiffs of herbed smoke into his lungs, easing his pain when his brow wrinkled at the stinging touch of each stitch.

When the back of his head was finished, the two men turned him again. Adam covered Connor with a blanket from the nearby double bed, which stood nestled in the far corner of the room against one wall.

Adam carefully pulled the jagged cut on the forehead together, sealing the edges with small, neat stitches. Sweat gleamed on his massively muscled body. Rivulets ran off his wide shoulders and dripped from his angular face onto Connor's chest, pooling in the dip of his sternum and gathering in the hollow of his throat, each drop marking Connor with his scent.

Adam worked in measured, unhurried precision. He kept one hand on Connor's cheek, fingers stroking over the pale skin, imparting comfort and reassurance that he was near, imprinting his touch and scent on the unconscious mind of his chosen mate.

Finished, Adam trimmed the thread with his knife and allowed the shaman to apply a layer of salve from a clay pot to the wound.

The fire crackled loudly, the flames increased and the shadows leapt higher with them. Several wolves could be heard howling nearby and the blustering winds blew under the door only to be forced back by the heat of the room and the dancing shadows.

Removing the blanket, Adam picked Connor up from the table, his body bending and flexing with an ease and grace of a wild beast, all restrained power and unimaginable strength. In rhythm with the shaman's chant, wisps of black shadow circled around him, encouraging, guiding, and leading the way, all at once. He cradled Connor to his chest like a sleeping child, cautiously supporting his head on one shoulder, and carried him to the waiting bed.

Pulling back the well worn, but serviceable blankets, he lowered his naked mate onto the mattress. Arranging Connor on his right side, Adam turned his head so that no pressure was on the wounds.

Adam tugged the covers over Connor's waist, then sat down on the bed beside him, his gaze never leaving Connor's face. He leaned down to nuzzle Connor's jaw, sniffing and rubbing his cheek over the angle of his jaw, lightly licking the thin skin behind Connor's ear, tasting him.

The chanting receded, then faded altogether. The shadows slowly retreated from around the couple as the ancient call died away. In the sudden silence, only the faint whish of the winds outside and the occasional pop from the fireplace could be heard.

The shaman replaced his medicines in the pouch and placed it under the table again, within easy reach. "He needs rest and warmth. Nourish him, both in body and spirit, young one. Even as he slumbers, his confused spirits search for reassurance. Be sure you are the one they find." Dyami slipped the robe from his shoulders and replaced it on the hook.

Adam nodded silently, still mesmerized by the man in his bed.

At the door, the shaman watched as the bright sapphire aura only he could see surrounded the newly mated pair, enfolding both men in its glow. His ancient face, seamed and heavily shadowed by the firelight, creased as he smiled, showing a flash of white.

"The spirits have chosen wisely. Now that our alpha leader has finally found his mate and is at peace, the spiritwalkers will rest and the pack will be whole once again. I will go and thank the spirits, and let the rest of the pack rejoice in the blessings of the day. Tonight, our hills will be alive with wolf songs."

Shifting into his werewolf form, the ancient shaman slipped away as quietly as he had entered. Adam barely noticed.

Attention riveted on Connor, Adam filtered out all the distractions in the room. Singing softly under his breath, he called to his own spirit totem to guide him. The strength of his animal spirit, the wolf who had created him, coursed through his already powerful body, calming him and allowing him to see into Connor's soul.

Thrilled by the twin spirits he sensed in the young doctor, Adam tenderly smoothed strands of hair off Connor's face, marveling at the soft texture on his rough, but sensitive fingertips. He held one lock of hair, turning it in the firelight, watching the way the strands changed from yellow to white to silvery gold. He patted it back into place, threading his hand into the downy thickness.

Dragging his fingers out of Connor's hair, Adam let his hand trail down the man's face, mapping the curve of his pale cheek, and the angle of his smooth jaw, then traced the soft fullness of his parted lips.

He lingered at Connor's mouth, letting the soft puffs of breath float over his fingertips, warming them. At the same time, Adam's other hand moved forward to rest on Connor's chest, the beating of his heart pulsing against his rib cage in mute reassurance. Adam reveled in the sensations on his hands, feeling the life forces of his chosen mate.

Eyes closed, and breathing deeply, he began to explore Connor's body, lightly outlining the shape of his neck and shoulder, touching the dip in his throat where his own sweat had pooled and dried, the finely muscled chest and lean trunk that tapered to a small waist. He stayed above the blanket, content for now to familiarize himself with the feel of Connor's skin and his distinctive scent.

Slowly sliding his hand down one pliant arm, he raised Connor's hand to his mouth. He nuzzled it, kissed the slightly curled fingers open, then licked his palm, savoring the taste, allowing Connor's flavor to imprint on him, forever ingraining the sight, scent, feel and taste in his heart and on his senses.

Lacing the fingers of their hands together, eyes still closed, Adam sat perfectly still on the bed, letting the spiritwalkers come back to him. They rejoiced in his finding his intended mate and, for a moment, he was transported into their world, spirits soaring and soul renewed.

A twitching in the hand laced with his abruptly brought Adam back to the real world of his small cabin. He opened his eyes to be greeted by a pair of dull, heavy-lidded, confused, green eyes trying hard to focus on him.

***

Chapter Five

The gray sky was heavy with clouds, their thick, dark billows blocking most of the dim morning light from the sheltered, little gully. Beyond the border of trees, the winds howled a mournful, tempestuous song that seemed to call out to the heavens. They swept the top layer of existing snow off the ground and whirled it through the air only to dust it over new rocks and tree limbs again and again.

In the small clearing under one mound of recently deposited snow, lay the exposed frame of a snow machine, bent handlebars bearing its weight as it lay on its side, half buried and silent.

With an explosive burst of force, the winds suddenly changed direction to barrel down into the thin strip of clearing, buffeting everything in their path.

Whipping across the underbelly of the dead machine, the winds dragged away layer after layer of snow until the machine was nearly exposed, revealing the human body huddled up under the protective frame. The winds pulled and plucked at the frozen sealskin parka, until finally it stirred on its own.

Limbs stiff and heavy, Dark slowly rolled onto his back, the movement reminding him of the location of each broken bone and frozen, bruised muscle. The pain would have been agonizing if not for the freezing temperature that numbed it all to a dull burn just hot enough to keep him conscious.

His left arm was broken in two places, the

grinding sensation just above his elbow making him grit
his teeth, while the dull, numbing throb in his wrist
made his hand essentially useless. His ribs along his
left side were cracked, some broken, and a stabbing
pain met each breath he forced into his lungs.

His left knee was tight and impossible to bend,
but the pain was less than in his arm and chest. A
manageable burn, but he couldn't tolerate any weight
on it. Blood had congealed on his face, frozen in the
creases and lines of his leathery skin, a by-product of
the deep gash between his eyes that ran from his
hairline to the end of his nose.

Slowly pulling himself up to one knee, inch by
agonizing inch, Dark clung to the snow machine for
support and protection as the winds battered against
him, trying to keep him down. Once steady, he used
the force of the wind as an aid while he rocked the snow
machine, trying to right its slightly battered frame back
onto its treads.

Again and again, Dark rammed the padded seat
with the bulk of his body, left side turned to the
numbing chill of the powerful winds. He was forced to
stop periodically to catch his breath and clear the
dizziness blurring his vision, but determination spurred
him on. He knew his path didn't include dying in this
frozen gully. He was part of a greater destiny. A life
depended on him, one he had sworn to guide and
protect.

Connor was marked by the moon, his fate
forever tied to the beast who had hunted them down
and taken him. But Dark knew Connor wasn't ready.
The spirits had moved too soon. He hadn't done his job

well enough yet.

Dark had lingered, enjoying the young man's company as he delayed in his teachings, telling only enough to spark interest, but not enough to give true understanding to the man. He had been afraid the intelligent, young doctor would see the true meaning of his tales too quickly and run from his destiny before the spirits were ready. Now it was he who had miscalculated and moved too slowly. The young doctor would be claimed and taken, transformed and forever locked into a world for which he wasn't prepared.

Dark had failed Connor once; he wouldn't fail him again. The full moon was days away. If he could alert the others, and retrieve the doctor, just for a few days, he could make him understand his role in the path chosen for him decades ago. Without understanding, the young man would be lost, overwhelmed and resistant to his new life.

Renewing his efforts, Dark pushed harder, letting all his pent-up anxiety and worry fuel his thrusts. The machine rocked and teetered on one thick, rubber tread, then slammed down to the snow, upright if slightly contorted.

Leaning on the seat, Dark folded into a huddle behind the shelter of the machine and took time to regain his strength, panting heavily into the cold air, each breath agony to his injured ribcage. A frosty mist clung to his eyebrows and the fur that edged the hood of his parka. Exhausted and in pain, he stayed that way for nearly half an hour before the bitter winds forced him into action again.

Clamping his useless left arm to his chest, Dark

grabbed the handlebar and heaved to his right knee, grimacing as his weight stressed the swollen flesh of his left leg. The feeling in his foot and lower leg were all but gone.

He gained the seat in a slow, awkward slide of stiff limbs and frozen clothing. Pawing at the dashboard, fingers numb despite his fur mittens, he was relieved to find the key still in the ignition.

The machine was new, the top of the line arctic model Greg had insisted on buying. It was extra large, extra heavy, with added fuel storage and an extra-heavy duty, subzero-tolerant battery. Dark had thought them extravagant when Greg had insisted on purchasing the machines, but now he gave a prayer of thanks to the spirits guiding the materialistic man.

Turning the key, he murmured another type of prayer and pleaded for the cold engine to kick over. Three agonizing tries later, the engine ground out a weak protest and caught. A loud roar of mechanical life shattered the calm of the gully and made Dark's spirit soar. Even the winds responded, pulling at his hunched back, slowing his already sluggish pace.

Easing the fuel lever forward with his right thumb, he maneuvered one-handed, forsaking the use of the brake on the left side for a moderate speed he could control with the gas feed.

The trail was uneven and difficult to see in the dim light and blowing snow. Dark had to stop time and time again to check his bearing or to rest. The muscles of his neck and shoulders, warmed by the physical strain of keeping the snow machine on track with one arm, screamed out their displeasure by cramping and twitching, hunched against the cold and wind.

By evening, Dark stopped and slumped down onto the wide seat, exhausted. He let the engine idle, resting, loathe to waste the gas, but even more afraid of shutting off the engine and risking it not starting again. The chill factor had increased and ice hung from the sides of the machine and his clothing. Fire burned across his shoulders and down deep into his lungs, the bite of the freezing air finally taking its toll on his waning stamina.

He had been traveling all day, closer and closer to town, covering mile after mile at a snail's pace. He struggled with the rough terrain, battling the pull and strain of the one-handed steering. Energy drained from his body along with the dropping temperatures. In the distance, he could just see the lights of Nekenano less than two miles away. Two, long, unobtainable miles away.

Finally giving into shock, Dark closed his eyes. He hugged the padded seat to his side to support his now lifeless arm, dimly aware of the creeping chill invading him, leeching the life from his entire body. The dim horizon faded from his sight only moments before the headlights of two snow machines picked up his hunched silhouette against the sky.

***

"Is he going to make it, Doc?" Mitch kept his distance from Dark's bedside, giving Pierce and Webb room to examine the battered man.

"He made it back on his own, and survived four

hours of surgery, he'll make it the rest of the way. He's strong."

Turning off his pocket flashlight, Greg released Dark's eyelid and leaned back, body perched on the edge of the sleek hospital bed. His back was rigid and the frown was back between his brows, furrowing his forehead.

Webb stood at Greg's shoulder, eyes clinically evaluating the unconscious man on the bed as she talked. "Strong enough to live through five fractured ribs, a punctured lung, two compound fractures in his arm, a broken knee cap and a concussion?"

Webb's scratchy, nasal voice made Greg's teeth ache. She sounded like she had polyps the size of peas on her vocal cords. He guessed the pack and a half of cigarettes she'd smoked daily since she arrived probably had something to do with it.

Mitch remained in the open doorway to the six-bed ward, watching Greg work. Greg glanced at Mitch, then flashed Webb a disapproving frown before looking back down at Dark.

"You don't know him. One of the first things you'll learn during your stay, Dr. Webb, is that the people here have an inner strength and fortitude you and I could only try to imagine."

His voice held a tinge of admiration in it when he continued. "I couldn't have survived these injuries, on my own, out there in the night for thirty-six hours, let alone make my way back to town in his condition. Could you?"

"Survive? Probably not. But neither has he -- yet."

"No faith in my surgical skills, Doctor?" Greg let enough sarcasm into his voice to let her know her opinion wouldn't faze him in the least one way or the other.

"On the contrary, from what I saw in the operating room a few hours ago, you're an amazing surgeon." She gestured vaguely in Dark's direction. "I'm just being realistic, Doctor."

"Well, don't be. He'll make it." Greg pushed off the bed and arched his back, taking satisfaction from each snap and pop of his vertebrae. Standing in surgery for hours, repairing shattered bones and mending a punctured lung had taken its toll on his energy.

"I think we can drop the formalities, too." Greg glanced at his new colleague and forced a smile, resigned to Webb's presence for the next six months. He was going to need someone to manage the clinic while they looked for Connor and she was the only game in town. "After all, we just spent hours sweating together in a life and death situation." He gave her one of his most charming smiles. "You can call me Greg."

Webb's answering grin was wry, but he could tell she was swayed by his charm and physical appeal.

"I don't think the OR counts as battlefield conditions, but fine." Her spine relaxed a fraction and her voice lost a little of the whine Greg found so grating. "Call me Ash."

"Good." He held her gaze for a moment longer. "You did a great job in surgery. I know you'll have no problem looking after things for the next day or so on your own."

He adjusted one of the IV lines and tucked in the

blanket around Dark's still body. "The day nurses, Emily and Rose, can give you a hand getting organized and finding things. They've been here since we opened."

Unfolding her arms, Webb frowned and gestured toward the outer hallway and the clinic beyond the ward. "Hey, wait a minute. I just got here. Where are you going?"

Greg barely glanced up at her. "Come first light, out to find Connor."

Stepping around the corner of the bed, Webb planted herself in front of the wires and tubes Greg was fussing with, forcing him to look at her. "You're a doctor. Aren't there search parties, policemen, for that kind of thing?"

Greg jerked his head toward Dark. "Take a look at the man in that bed, Ash. Connor was with him. What do you think *he'll* look like when we find him?"

Webb grimaced and sighed, but stared Greg in the eyes, challenging him to tell her she was wrong. "And what are you going to do for him out in the frozen tundra, miles from medical care?"

Never breaking the stare, Greg murmured, "More than I did the last time."

"What last time?" Webb frowned, the corners of her eyes wrinkling in confusion. "What are you talking about?"

"Never mind." Voice overly harsh, Greg broke the stare, his eyes darting first to Mitch's neutral, but ever-watchful face, then back to Webb. He sighed and softened his tone. "Long story, bad ending. And no, I won't tell you about it sometime."

A low groan and the rustle of crisp sheets drew their attention back to the bed. Greg surged forward and leaned over Dark, watching intently as the man twitched and rolled his head. The guide's dark eyes slowly fluttered open to meet Greg's.

"Dark? Can you hear me? It's Greg, Dr. Pierce."

Recognizing the dull, glazed stare caused by the after effects of anesthesia, Greg gave the man time to orient himself. When the dark eyes cleared to their usual sharp glare, he reached out and clasped Dark's arm, letting the man know he was real and not some shock-induced hallucination.

"You're home, back at the clinic. We, Dr. Webb and I, took you to surgery. You're going to be fine." The soft, familiar pad of worn boots told him the other guide had moved closer. "Mitch is here, too."

Dark hesitated, than carefully turned his head as he looked at the empty beds surrounding him.

"Where's the boy?" His lips barely moved and his words rasped painfully out of a dry throat.

Greg felt the muscles under his hand tense. "You mean Connor?"

Dark nodded once, then grimaced, pain etched in the deep lines around his mouth and eyes.

"We don't know where he is, Dark." Greg was surprised to hear his voice tremble. He drew in a deep breath and waited for a moment before continuing, pleased he sounded more in control when he spoke again.

"Mark and Beth Peters found you just outside of town around sundown." He patted the man's good arm. "You just spent the last couple of hours in surgery." He tightened his grip, and the guide opened his eyes again to focus on him. "What happened out there? Can you remember anything?"

Glancing off to a point somewhere over Greg's shoulder, Dark's gaze grew unfocused and distant. After a few seconds his eyes cleared and he snapped his gaze back to Greg's, a combination of remorse and awe on his face.

"A skinwalker... took him." Dark paused, breathing heavily. "A wolf... knocked us from the sled... and... and a bigger one carried him away."

"A what?" Greg shook his head and snorted a sharp, indignant sound. "What do you mean 'took him'? A wolf can't carry a full-grown man away."

The injured man's head sunk back into the pillow, his face more ashen than before.

Greg lightly shook Dark's shoulder. "A skinwalker? Are you talking about a spirit? A spirit took Connor?"

"What's he talking about? What's a skinwalker?" Webb looked to Greg and when he ignored her, she turned to Mitch for an answer.

Quietly, Mitch stepped forward. "A skinwalker is an ancient belief of our people, a night guardian, a child of the moon. If it comes in the form of a wolf, in your language, he would be called a... a werewolf."

"You're not serious." Webb snorted and folded her arms across her chest while taking a step away from the bed. Her eyes darted from one man to the next.

Frowning, Greg sat back and released his hold on Dark. "Of course, he's not serious." He gestured at the heavy bandages encircling Dark's head. "The man has a concussion, for Christ's sake. He's probably been hallucinating for the last two days." Then a little more uncertainly he added, "He's just confused."

Opening his eyes again, Dark visibly strained to keep awake. "But my eyes still work, Dr. Pierce." His quiet confidence sent a chill through Greg. "A skinwalker has claimed him, taken him to the spirit world." Dark's eyes fluttered closed and he seemed to fall asleep again.

The room fell silent. Webb ran her hands up and down her arms as if to warm them and stepped closer to the doorway.

Greg and Mitch traded stares until Mitch broke the silence. "I did find tufts of fur on the handlebars of the snow machine when I looked it over. There was a wolf there."

That took the wind out of Greg's argument that the man was hallucinating, at least about the wolf attack.

"That still doesn't make sense," Greg huffed. "You know as well as I do, that wolves wouldn't come anywhere near a running snow machine. It's too big."

"Why not? They run down moose and they're bigger than a sled."

Worry mounting, Greg's voice rose. "For God's sake, Mitch, moose don't make the kind of noise one of those damn machines do." His raised voice stirred the man on the bed.

Dark rallied, one hand reaching up to clasp Greg's wrist. "It is the truth. The boy is with his skinwalker." He shook his head and a single tear slid down the side of his weathered face. His voice grew faint and jumbled. "Too soon, too soon. I didn't tell him enough. He won't understand the path he is destined to walk."

Greg grasped the dark-skinned fingers wrapped tightly around his wrist and held on, trying to silently reassure the distraught man. "It'll be all right, you're just a little confused by everything that's happened." Dark's eyes reluctantly fluttered and closed. "Rest."

Greg stared at Dark, trying to imagine what the man would have seen out there that would have given him the impression of a werewolf, but rational thought kept intruding. "He must have seen someone else out there."

"Who would be out there, in the middle of nowhere?" Shivering noticeably, Webb grabbed a blanket from a nearby linen cart and placed it over Dark's chest. She took another one and wrapped it around her own shoulders, covering the short sleeves of the thin, scrub top.

"There is one possibility, Doc." Mitch moved to the end of the bed and watched his friend drift off to sleep, putting an end to any more answers they were going to get from him. "There is a small tribe that lives north of Raven Gully, an isolated Dena'ina settlement. They are known for avoiding others outside their tribe. If they had come across the accident, they would have taken Dr. Jacy there."

"Really?" Greg stood up, slowly slipping his hand from Dark's now lax grip. He turned to face Mitch, happy to have something to latch onto. "I didn't know there was a settlement that far out."

Greg frowned, then the furrows marking his

forehead smoothed out in relief. "But that's good. At least there's the possibility Connor got help, that he's not lying out there frozen to death, or being used as a meal for the scavengers." Greg stood up straighter, his mouth pressed into a firm line. "He's not dead if someone carried him away."

"Why leave Dark behind?" Webb asked.

"Maybe they thought he was dead." Mitch stared down at his counterpart. Dark's chest rose and fell in a shallow rhythm and he groaned softly in his sleep.

Webb glanced at the still, ashen-faced man covered in casts and bandages, a chest tube running from his left side to a container on the floor. "Well, he certainly *looked* dead when he got here."

"Maybe. It would make sense." Greg glanced at Dark, then began pacing in the narrow space between the beds, his pace increasing with each word he spoke. "Doesn't matter now. He's here and on the mend. And now we have an idea of where to look for Connor. That's what matters. Finding Connor and making sure he's all right."

Mitch moved to the doorway with the same energy of purpose that had taken over Greg. "I will make sure the search team is ready."

"Yes." Greg pointed his finger at Mitch and began ticking off items on his fingertips. "Two medical packs and all the portable drugs including supplies for transfusions. Extra blankets, and tell Emily to make sure no sulfa drugs are in the kit. Connor's allergic to them. I want to leave as soon as it's light enough to see the trail, Mitch. Not one minute later. We still don't know how badly he's hurt."

Mitch nodded and disappeared down the hallway. Webb followed him out, saying, "I'll check on the drug packs for you."

Feeling a sudden, unexplainable loss when Mitch left the room, Greg tried to track the man by his footsteps, but the guide was too light on his feet. Greg suddenly realized how much he depended on Mitch, counted on him as a guide and as a friend. He had never thought of Mitch that way before. Actually, he didn't usually think about Mitch very often at all. Never had to, the man was always there.

Greg took another look at his friend on the bed and allowed himself a moment of satisfaction. He and Webb had saved Dark's life today. The older man would be able to return to his normal life in time. And now they needed time to find the other accident victim.

His thoughts turned immediately to Connor, overwhelmed by the fear the young man would be in worse shape than Dark had been. Greg sniffed and wiped at his eyes, forcing the terror of failure back into the dark place he always kept it, chained under a facade of casual indifference.

Looking out into the black night through the large window at one end of the room, Greg spoke out loud, defying anyone or anything that might be listening.

"I'm not losing this one, either."

***

By six o'clock the next morning, Mitch joined six

local volunteers, two police officers and Greg for the search.

The medical pack Greg had packed was so heavy Mitch had trouble lifting it onto the gurney sled being towed behind his snow machine.

Mitch noted the way conversation among the men was nearly non-existent, the group's mood somber. Word had traveled about the severity of Dark's injuries. The possibility they would find the well-liked young doctor in the same shape, or worse, was never far from their thoughts.

When the first rays of dull sunshine lightened the shroud of snow-filled clouds overhead, the ten men climbed aboard their machines and set out on the trail. The most experienced tracker in the group, Mitch naturally took the lead.

Changing his usual role of outspoken leader to quiet follower without complaint, Greg fell into position by Mitch's side.

Stealing a glance at Greg as the doctor pulled up beside him, Mitch gave him a quick nod, his eyes silently acknowledging the shift in their roles. Mitch took the moment to unexpectedly wink at the doctor, startling him. When Greg could only blink back in wide-eyed surprise, Mitch's lips twitched into a tiny, flirtatious smile and he roared off, the rest of the team following close behind.

***

Chapter Six

The pounding in his head made Connor's stomach roll. Behind his eyes, bright lights stabbed into his brain like a thousand tiny shards of broken glass. His limbs felt as if they were encased in lead. His body heavy and non-responsive, he felt a rush of panic constrict his throat.

He clenched his fists to help him roll to his side and unexpectedly gripped warm flesh beneath the fingers of one hand. Muscles twitching, Connor realized someone was holding his hand and he forced open leaden eyelids. Expecting to see Greg, his heart thundered in his chest when his blurry eyes saw only a large, dark, shadowy form leaning over him, holding on to him. It was too large to be Greg.

Disjointed memories flashed through his mind at high speed. The last thing he saw before passing out had been the glowing eyes and dark fur of some huge, wild animal. In the flickering, dim light cast by a blazing fire in the hearth on the opposite wall, the hulking body sitting next to him vaguely seemed to take on the same features. Mind racing and body resisting all his efforts to calm down, terror raced through him and Connor retched and heaved. The room swirled around him at a dizzying speed. The air seemed to evaporate from his lungs. He clenched his eyes closed in a vain attempt to stop the spinning motion. Blood pounded in his aching head and his mouth went dry. Spasm after spasm twisted through his violently rebelling stomach, emptying its entire contents.

The room spun again, this time in a different direction and Connor forgot about the creature beside him. He couldn't leave his eyes open. The lights behind them were blinding even without the added vibrant illumination of the fire. He vomited everything he had in his stomach, then moved on to dry heaving, barely able to draw a breath inbetween stomach convulsions. He felt as if his body was trying to eliminate every one of his vital organs out through his mouth. He didn't think the heaving would ever end.

Tears streamed down his cheeks and his nose dripped. He felt a few tiny blood vessels in his face rupture with the continual strain of heaving. The smell and taste of partially digested food and stomach acid filled his nostrils and mouth. It made his throat burn, and was strong enough to mask the scent of smoky wood in the warm room. Connor felt completely disconnected and out of synch with the world.

After what seemed like hours, the heaving slowed to a nauseous churning. Suddenly aware of the soft surface he was lying on, Connor began to relax his rigid, sore muscles. Gasping slightly, relieved to be able to breathe easier, he slowly began to roll onto his back. He found a heavy, hot pressure in the middle of his spine pushing back at him, gently forcing him to remain lying on his side. Too exhausted to fight, Connor gave in and stilled his movements, lying lax and unresisting in a tangle of unresponsive limbs.

Connor's mind drifted, his thoughts jumbled out of sequence, all mixed up with nightmare visions of ice, wolves and huge walking beasts. The thought of Dark briefly flashed across his mind and he knew he should be paying more attention, but he couldn't focus.

A moan escaped him and he immediately cut it off, the harsh acid burn in his throat too much to tolerate. The sound alerted whoever was with him, and a cool cloth was obligingly wiped over his sweaty, drool-covered face. His hair was cautiously patted back from his forehead, a few strands tugged painfully, matted to his skin for some reason.

The tugging sensation was minor, but the burst of pain it caused to shoot through his head was appalling. The rolling sense of nausea rocketed up from the depths of his sore stomach again and a sour taste made his jaw ache, a familiar warning he was about to vomit. He began heaving all over again, absurdly grateful he was still on his side. A quick peek through tear-filled, blurry eyes showed him he was heaving into a metal bucket held in place by a large, cinnamon-colored hand.

Somewhere between the tenth and twentieth time he vomited, Connor risked tilting his face up and stole a glance at his silent, steadfast guardian angel. The dim vision of kind, dark eyes set in a handsome, chiseled, Native American face atop a heavily muscled, naked chest registered for all of three seconds before a fresh wave of vomiting began, pulling his attention away.

When the last wave died away, Connor slumped down, head hanging over the edge of the bed, too exhausted to open his eyes. As if in some distant dream, he could feel his body being repositioned. He was naked and covered in sweat. The smell of old blood near his nose made his stomach roll. His face felt stiff in places, as if pancake syrup had dried on his skin. His eyelids felt too heavy to move, each fine blond eyelash having turned into a lead weight.

Feeling worse than he had felt in his entire life, Connor lost all desire to do anything other than sleep. A sudden, nagging worry he wouldn't wake up if he was left alone gripped him. He moved restlessly in the bed, a small whimper escaping his dry, cracked lips. One hand clenched and unclenched, twisting the blanket covering his flushed body, while the other searched the surface looking for something substantial to latch onto. His questing hand bumped into a mass of solid warmth. Stout fingers gripped his wrist, stopping the restless movement, then laced between his own fingers, holding on tightly.

Connor sighed in relief. The painful, swirling visions in his head faded, their colors and sounds suddenly muted, receding to the background of his mind.

He entertained a fevered wish that if the wolf beast he had seen earlier was going to devour him, it would do it quickly and soon. Very soon.

His thoughts dwindled to nothingness as a dense cloud of lethargy descended and sleep claimed him, his hand still tightly entwined with the protective presence at his side.

***

Waking the second time was better, but not by much. The air smelled faintly of old blood, sweat and burning wood, all of them objectionable to Connor's raw throat and sore stomach. Without opening his eyes, he recognized the sounds of fierce winter winds rattling glass windowpanes.

Connor awoke only because his body demanded it. His mouth was so parched his tongue was stuck to the roof of his mouth. His lips cracked and split when he tried to lick them. His throat was swollen and raw, making him imagine what it would be like to sip battery acid. The churning nausea in his gut had finally settled down to a rolling queasiness. But the slightest movement of his head seemed to stir the contents of his stomach and set off a fireworks display of pain in the back of his skull.

Eyelids still heavy and crusted over with sleep, Connor forced them open to half-mast, not even bothering to try to focus on anything. He experimentally clenched one hand, a foggy memory of earlier warmth cradling it stuck in his mind, but he found only soft, worn fabric beneath his palm. He turned his head slightly towards the bright glow of light in the room and the nausea exploded into gut wrenching pain.

Gagging, powerless to move, Connor started at the sight of a large, dark shadow swooping down on him. Strong arms lifted his upper torso up, cradling him, while a solid, hot wall of flesh sat down behind him, supporting him.

"Oh, God, stop!" Connor cried out as the swift movements intensified his distress, but the person holding him paid no attention, firmly holding his head to one side as he vomited.

After what seemed like forever, a fresh cool cloth dabbed at his face. One corner of the wet cloth was pressed to his dry lips, and then the edge was slipped into his mouth and squeezed. A trickle of cool water dribbled onto his tongue. Connor latched onto it and feebly sucked at it, savoring every droplet of moisture. His stomach rolled in protest, but his mouth was so parched it was all absorbed before he could swallow any of it. The cloth was wet again and again for him until his nausea finally swelled to intolerance and Connor reluctantly heeded the warning.

Relaxing more fully into the support at his back, Connor turned his head to one side and his cheek met flesh. He slowly realized his bare back was plastered to equally bare skin and a man was firmly holding him. Gasping with the effort, he forced his eyes open a bit more and eased his head back.

Sight blurred by tears from vomiting and double vision he knew was a side effect of the blinding headache he had, Connor laid back against the hard shoulder and turned his face up. He forced his eyes to focus on the outline above him.

What drew his attention first were the man's eyes. They were as black and as deep as a starless night. The man cocked his head to one side, seemingly to give Connor a better view. For a brief instant, Connor thought the dark eyes shone a rusty orange. Startled, Connor blinked and stared, then gave an embarrassed huff. He imagined his own green eyes were illuminated oddly, caught in the same yellow and orange light from the blazing fireplace.

Mesmerized by the color change, Connor looked

deeper into the dark orbs. Their gentle, almost awe-filled expression gave him an instant sense of security and belonging. Whomever this man was caring for him, he was tender and gentle in a manner that contradicted the large, hulking build and rough hands Connor could now feel cautiously massaging his churning stomach muscles in an effort to relax them.

Long, black hair framed the man's dark face, and a glint of silver in it danced in the dim light when he moved.

As he stared at the man, one coarse palm slid up Connor's chest and over his neck to rest on his temple. The man's fingers gently combed his hair off his face, then moved down to trace the outline of his cheekbone. Connor found the soft, repetitive motion both soothing and distracting, almost loving. He realized it was a familiar touch, a touch he knew from his frequent dreams.

Connor licked at his parched lips, noticing the sensitive tissues were now coated with a thin layer of something thick and greasy, though not unpleasant. His voice was barely more than a soft croak through hoarse vocal cords. "Where am I?"

"Safe," came the simple answer, spoken in a rich, deep voice that made Connor's heart skip a beat.

Connor reached up to touch the painful spot on his forehead, fingers clumsily examining the rough suture line. "What happened?"

"You hit your head." Connor's heart jumped again at the sound.

A strong, gentle hand stopped him from fingering the wound. Connor squinted up to get a better look at the man. "Do I... know you?"

The dark head nodded. Silver flashed in the firelight, creating ribbons of moonbeams on the walls.

The gentle, deep voice softly whispered in his ear. "Yes, adada. I live here," the man touched Connor's chest just over his left breast, "in your heart."

Convinced this was all a dream, Connor fumbled a hand up off the bed and touched the heavily muscled arm resting on his stomach, trailing his fingers along its width to the thick, strong wrist. He gripped the wrist with his hand, finding it impossible to encircle it more than part way with his fingers. Without releasing his grip, he closed his eyes and settled back onto the hard chest. "I must have... a bigger heart... than I thought."

A deep chuckle rumbled up from the depths of the man's chest and echoed through Connor's back, vibrating down his spine. "Very big, adada, very big."

Connor clenched his ass to stop the flow of an electric sensation sizzling through him before it landed in his groin and awakened a need he wasn't remotely prepared to meet.

Blinking hard to clear his vision to take one last good look at his guardian angel, Connor was struck by two thoughts. The first was that lying in this man's arms felt very right, like he was born to be here. The second was that of all the possible saviors his jumbled, fevered mind could have produced, he was glad it had picked the handsome, exotic lover from his recent fantasies.

Content with his dream, he turned his face into the crook of the man's brawny neck, then sighed and let the heavy pull of sleep claim him again.

***

The swish and gurgle of warm water running through his hair revived his senses the next time Connor woke. The water trickled down the back of his neck while blunt fingers massaged his scalp, washing away the stink of sweat and dried blood.

He tried to move his arms and found them locked to his sides, his entire body wrapped in a thin blanket. Connor shivered as more warm water cascaded over his hair and down around his ears, tickling the sensitive skin behind them.

Connor moved restlessly, a thousand questions taking form in his slowly clearing mind. He opened his mouth, trying to moisten his lips and free his dry tongue. Before he could form a coherent word, a dime-sized chunk of something solid and cold was wordlessly eased between his parted lips.

From the grainy consistence, he realized it was snow. The moisture and the cold were a godsend to his dehydrated body. When his stomach accepted the first few swallows without immediately rebelling, Connor eagerly sucked on it, forgetting everything else. A second piece followed the first.

Feeling partially revived, his eyes opened to small slits and he looked at the room from upside down. His fantasy man was still at his side. Connor could feel the heat of his body and the brush of the tips of his long hair over Connor's bare shoulders as he worked.

"You are awake again, adada."

Connor looked up to see dark eyes and a slight smile on the man's upside down face. The stranger was still an amazing sight -- tall, handsome and built -- just like in his dreams. His impressive chest was still bare, but his lower half was clad in soft, buckskin pants.

The hands washing him felt solid and the deep, soothing tones of the man's voice seemed to vibrate through his fingertips into Connor's body. He was beginning to think that maybe he wasn't dreaming after all. The dull, aching pain in his head felt too real.

Connor licked his lips and cleared his raw throat twice before any sound would come out. "You keep calling me that, 'adada'. My name is Connor, Connor Jacy." He paused for a breath, clearing his throat again. Even then it was hoarse and barely audible. "I'm a doctor at the clinic in… Nekenano."

"Adada means 'dear one' in my language. You are a healer, a medicine man, and a two spirit. You are very dear."

"What's a… two spirit?" Connor's voice faded on the last syllable.

The man continued gently washing Connor's hair as he explained. "Within your soul dwells both a male and a female spirit. It gives you twice the strength and lets you see people differently than others." He stopped and stared down into Connor's face. "The female spirit within you allows you to be attracted to men. Men like me."

Connor gasped and looked away, but his eyes betrayed him and quickly flickered back to Adam's dark, intense gaze.

Adam's expression became solemn, but his eyes shone brightly, a new sense of awe in them. "The spirits have seen fit to bestow a great many blessings on my house."

The fingertips of one hand ghosted over Connor's temple, the touch reverent. He locked gazes with Connor and said, "I am called Adam."

The man's name was spoken low and sensually, presented like a gift. A shiver slithered through Connor's lean frame at the sound of it. He felt as if a part of Adam's soul had just been given to him. It excited and thrilled him, stirring an electric sensation deep in his chest and groin. Throat tight with unexpected emotion, his gaze remained riveted to Adam's dark eyes.

"Adam. I like that. Fits you."

Sitting beside Connor on the bed, Adam worked his fingers through the doctor's blond strands one last time, squeezing the excess water out. He took great care at the back of Connor's head, but Connor still gasped and went rigid when the base of his skull was touched. The pain sparked memories, and flashes of the accident came rushing down on Connor. He suddenly knew this wasn't a dream. Panicked, he looked for reassurance and answers from Adam.

"What happened? How did I get here? Where's Dark?"

The pain was real, Adam was real, and Connor had no idea how or why he was in this cabin, isolated, injured and alone with this stranger. Anxiety poured over him and he broke out in a cold sweat. Vision both blurred and doubled, his eyes darted over the tiny cabin looking for the missing guide.

"Where's Dark? Where's my guide, the man who was with me?" Connor struggled with the blanket wrapped around him, but a strong restraining hand prevented him from removing it.

"You were unconscious on the ground, next to your snow machine. You had suffered two blows to your head, one here," he touched Connor's forehead and the doctor flinched, "and here." Adam moved his fingers to touch the edge of the swollen, painful area on the back of Connor's skull where he had struck the ice. "The old one with you was too badly injured. The spirit world called to him."

Connor stilled and stared at Adam's face, letting the solemn words sink into his foggy brain. His voice came out as a whisper when he found the energy to speak. "He's dead? Dark's dead?"

Nodding, Adam squeezed Connor's arm. "The loss saddens you."

"He was a… a friend, a good friend." Connor felt a sudden emptiness in his chest, a new ache to add to his growing list of discomforts. Tears burned at the back of his eyes. "I'll…I'll miss him."

Adam reached out and tilted Connor's chin up so that their eyes meet.

"He will live on then, in your heart, adada." Adam tapped his own chest over his left breast. "The spirits will guide him on his new path. He will not be alone. It is the way of our people."

Adam shifted position and his large hand protectively cupped the back of Connor's neck just below the painful area.

Connor gasped and stiffened slightly when Adam effortlessly lifted him and repositioned him on the bed, his damp head gently cradled and then lowered to a soft pillow. Connor had trouble keeping his eyes off Adam's strong, chiseled face, a little unnerved by the man's power and grace.

"I hit my head? Is that all?" Connor took stock of the aches and pains in his body. He began clinically checking off a mental list of possible problems from the clues his body was giving him, but his battered brain just wasn't up to the challenge yet. Connor's thoughts swirled and his throat tightened. Tears of frustration and uncertainty welled up and he had to swallow several times to keep a lump from forming in his throat. He coughed, choking the tears back, determined to stay in control of himself.

Sitting down on the bed beside Connor, Adam softly told him, "You have a head injury. You have been vomiting and sleeping for a full day. The wounds were not deep, but the blows that caused them were harsh."

Fresh memories lit up Connor's pain-dulled eyes. "A wolf... a wolf rushed us, knocked us from the sled. Dark lost control and... and...." A lost expression fell across Connor's face and he blinked several times to try and clear the haze of uncertainty clouding his memory. "I don't know what happened after that. I've been dreaming and seeing things and... and nothing seems real to me right now."

"I am real, Connor." Adam gently stroked the side of Connor's face. The warm touch calmed Connor and anchored him to the here and now, more reassuring

81

than mere words did.

Adam began to unwrap the blanket from around Connor's body. He took his time, gently bathing him a portion at a time. His hands were rough, but Connor found the steady touch soothing.

Too tired and weak to object, Connor resigned himself to letting Adam do the job, anxious to get rid of the stink of old blood and stale body odor. He relaxed into the delicious feelings of the warm water, slick soap and solid, firm strokes on his skin. Unexpectedly, he felt his groin tighten, his cock hardening slightly at the sensual attention.

Eyes darting distractedly from object to object around the room, Connor tried to concentrate on first the fireplace and then the sparse furniture in the room, but his eyes ended back up on Adam.

Connor first noticed the way Adam adorned parts of his long, black hair. Two small sections were braided on the left, while one on the right side of his face was merely wrapped with leather laces. Two wide, engraved silver bands were intricately woven into the leather and secured to the thick lock of hair. Fascinated by their native designs, Connor reached out and lightly touched them.

"These are beautiful. I think I know them, the patterns I mean." It took a moment, but he finally recognized it. "There's a totem outside the clinic with them on it. Greg… a friend of mine, said it was new, erected right before I came to the clinic. It has these same patterns on it." It was a great honor for the clinic to have received it from the native community of the town, and Connor knew Greg was very proud of it.

He let the bands slip through his fingers, savoring the coolness of the metal against his fevered hand.

"Dark...," Connor had to swallow hard before he could continue, "Dark said the patterns represented ancient spirits, some legendary guardians of the night. Others were healing spirits, nurturers of earth's creatures, like doctors. He told me it was an unusual combination on a totem, but I think they go well together."

The silver bands caught the gleam of the fire, their polished surface and cut edges illuminated to a soft, white glow. Connor's eyes were immediately drawn back to them, and from there, his gaze flickered to Adam's mouth.

Adam's bottom lip was dark pink and plump, his upper one slightly thinner, with defined peaks that lined up under his nostrils. As the man continued washing Connor, he occasionally drew his lower lip in and moistened it with his tongue. Between the warm glide of the soapy cloth and Adam's highly seductive presence, Connor was having trouble keeping his thoughts and his body's reactions from turning sexual. He was injured, hundreds of miles from town, and grieving for a lost friend, but the attraction for this quiet, powerful man was almost overwhelming.

Adam finished washing Connor from the waist up, and Connor thought he was done until the blanket was calmly folded back, revealing the rest of his naked body.

Connor gasped at the suddenness, and his half-hard cock expanded a bit more. It was impossible to hide and Connor didn't have the energy or the desire to make an excuse for it. He darted a worried glance at Adam, uncertain if the man was offended by his obvious attraction to him.

The corners of Adam's mouth twitched, but he just continued to wash over Connor's stomach and down his legs, avoiding the problem area.

While his hands worked, Adam's eyes wandered up to meet Connor's worried gaze. Adam smiled and said, "The rest of your body seems to be working just fine."

The cloth was discarded. Warm, soapy hands massaged the back of Connor's knees, then sauntered their way up his inner thighs.

Connor's voice was strained and husky, excited by the light, teasing touch. "I...I find you very... attractive. Obviously."

Smile turning seductive and pleased, Adam brought the washcloth back, its fresh warmth and soap-slicked, fabric-roughened surface adding a tantalizing mix of sensation to Connor's groin.

Adam's voice was low, rich and soothing. It flowed over Connor like warm honey. "The spirits have blessed us both then. I desire you greatly, as well."

Panting, Connor managed a small, "Oh."

The washcloth moved higher, slithering and tugging its way around Connor's hardening erection. Connor closed his eyes and grabbed Adam's wrist to stop him. "I'm...I'm not really... up for anything just now. I...I mean...well, I mean I couldn't...you wouldn't get anything out of --."

"Hush." Adam gently removed Connor's fingers from around his wrist and placed them on the mattress. "Now is for you, adada. Later, when you are better, there will be time for us. I will have all I need with your pleasure."

The cloth was replaced with Adam's large, slippery hands, his fingers firmly encasing the length of Connor's rock-hard cock. He slowly turned one hand one direction and the other hand the opposite, pumping and twisting up and down the shaft.

Connor arched his back and let the rough caress consume him as sensual delight tingled up his spine from his cock. A few short strokes and his skin felt like it was on fire. The dull ache in his head receded to the background and even his nausea settled down to a pale flutter. In no time at all, he was near orgasm.

"Oh, Jesus...I mean... Adam... I can't believe... believe I'm going to lose it already." The excitement of the mysterious, beautiful and exotic man was too much for Connor to hold back his response.

Adam kept his strokes rhythmic and firm, gliding his callused thumb around the rim of Connor's swollen cock head, teasing the sensitive underside with each upward pass. When Connor bit down on his lower lip in strained frustration, Adam swiftly leaned forward and sealed his mouth over one of Connor's nipples. He used his teeth to firmly anchor the swollen bud in place, then jabbed and stroked it with his tongue, biting down just enough to make Connor gasp and groan.

"Ugh! Ah! Augh!" Connor grunted at the sharp burn in his nipple, arching his chest up against

Adam's mouth. The movement tugged his hypersensitive tit against the sharp edges of the teeth holding it. Sizzling streaks of fire shot from the tender nub of flesh straight to his groin. Body dehydrated, Connor's cock exploded in a weak spray of cum.

Connor nearly blacked out from the rush. He lay weak and exhausted, mind floating in a thick blanket of swirling shadows. The faint pulse of muted, rhythmic drumming seemed to play in the far corners of his mind, an ancient beat both primal and ritualized.

In Connor's mind, shadows of the room ghosted closer, their indistinct forms vaguely resembling native warriors of a time past. As the drums grew in volume, the clearer the warriors became. Their painted faces and elaborate dress appeared stark against their warm, cinnamon skin and solemn faces. Just as the warriors began to chant, a splash of cool water flowed over Connor's spent shaft and groin, jarring him from his vision. Startled, Connor opened his eyes to watch Adam tenderly sponge the spent body fluids from his skin.

When he finished, Adam stood and bodily lifted Connor from the bed. Taken by surprise, Connor latched onto the man's wide shoulders, marveling at the feel of the smooth, warm flesh covering the solid, thick muscles of the man's impressive body.

Wide green eyes locked with unfathomable black ones and Connor closed the few inches between them, tentatively kissing Adam's hot, full lips. The tender kiss was modest and undemanding.

Pulling back, Connor gave Adam a shy, but sated smile and murmured, "Thank you. I…." He dropped his gaze for a second, then looked back up, unwilling to release the intense dark eyes from his own just yet. "Just… thank you. For everything, not just… now."

Adam returned the smile with a seductive tilt of head and a noticeable tightening of his hold on Connor's naked body. Never breaking the hold his eyes had on Connor's, his voice turned husky and deeper, claiming, "Pleasuring your body nurtures your spirits and mine." His smile grew a little more heated. "And know, the pleasure was mine, as well."

His smile widening, Connor relaxed back into the man's strong arms. A wave of heavy exhaustion washed over him. Suddenly, the roar of the winds outside the cabin grew louder and the glow of the blazing fire hurt his eyes. Connor grimaced, obviously reaching the end of his waning strength again.

Adam swiftly pulled the damp blanket off the bed, then settled Connor on the fresh sheets, careful to support and protect his injured head the entire time. His gaze lingered over Connor's body before he started to pull away. Connor's hand on his arm stopped him.

"You knew before you started washing me I was attracted to you, didn't you?" Connor could barely keep his eyes open. "How'd you know I'd be okay with a man touching me?"

Adam was silent, his eyes studying Connor's face, visually outlining old scars and the new one Connor would have when his current wound healed.

"I smelled another man on you." The pronouncement was flat and factual, his voice non-judgmental, but his tone held a definite edge of displeasure. "Not just his body scent. The scent of his lovemaking."

Connor's heavy lids blinked back open and his voice rose with each word. "You *smelled* him?"

Adam shrugged. "Best tracker in the territory." Adam tapped the side of his long, straight, bronzed nose, and breathed deeply. "Good sense of smell." Adam casually shrugged again. Dismissing the subject, he walked to the hearth and began banking the fire for the night.

Giving a small, surprised chuckle, Connor closed his tired eyes, then opened one back up to study his companion. "Was that the real reason for the bath? To get rid of the smell of another man?"

Clearing away the few items from the bath as he talked, Adam returned to the bed with a metal cup full of freshly melted snow water. Sitting down on the bed, he pulled Connor into a sitting position.

Connor gratefully accepted the cup. He let Adam help him drink and waited for an answer.

The seductive smile on Adam's face turned into a small smirk. "Washing away the past is a time honored ritual. The cleansing bath is the start of a new beginning."

Placing the empty cup on the table, he stood up and pulled at the ties at his waist, dropping the buckskin pants to the floor, then gracefully stepping out of them.

Connor's eyes popped open wider at the sight of the man's flaccid, but huge cock.

Ignoring Connor's speechless reaction, Adam walked to the bed and slid in under the covers.

"Besides, you smelled." He rolled on his side toward Connor and threw an arm over the other man's lean stomach. "And if I am to share my bed with you, you needed to smell better." Adam closed his eyes and pulled the blanket up to cover both of them.

Astounded by the man's casually dominant behavior, Connor remained silent while Adam settled in around him. Within moments, he felt even, regular breaths wafting across his bare chest. The stout arm across his middle was warm and surprisingly comfortable, reassuring and protective in a way no one else had ever made Connor feel.

This man, this burly, native tracker, his heroic rescuer, tender caregiver and possible future lover was a mystery, complex and exciting in a way that shook Connor's heart and rattled his senses. If he hadn't just met the man, he'd suspect he was falling in love.

The howling winds outside grew louder. The rising sound invaded Connor's thoughts and lulled his hazy mind toward sleep. Just as he dropped off, the arm around his waist tightened a fraction, and the winds took on a regular, thudding tempo that sounded faintly like native drums.

***

89

Chapter Seven

The snowstorm descended on the search team only a few hours after they left the safety of town. The fierce howling winds and driving snow forced the men to scramble for cover.

A seasoned hunter well acquainted with the area, Mitch led them to a small cave carved into a hillside not far from the trail they were on. He'd used it for shelter before, and a fair supply of dry wood and kindling were still present.

Once the men had a fire going, and enough additional wood gathered to keep them relatively warm during the night, they settled into a meal of dried beef, cold biscuits and hot coffee.

After pairing up in teams of two, the men took two hour shifts to tend the fire and make sure no wild animals joined them in their cozy retreat. Mitch paired with Greg, as usual. Greg was too tense and restless to sleep, so Mitch suggested they take the first shift.

The rest of the search party bedded down for the night. The fire was near the mouth of the cave's hollow for ventilation, the winds drawing the thick smoke out into the night and away from the confines of their small shelter. The majority of the men had unrolled their sleeping bags near the back, where the heat from the fire was trapped.

Sitting on tiny, collapsible campstools by the fire, Greg and Mitch shared their usual companionable silence. They had, over the years, become comfortable with the long, wordless stretches between them.

Greg stared out at the swirling curtain of white just outside the cave's mouth. It was snowing hard and blowing even harder, piling up in thick drifts against the hillside.

Greg started as Mitch gave voice to the same thought he was about to mention. "We'll have to spend an hour digging out the snow machines when this stops."

That seemed to be happening a lot lately. Either he was getting too predictable or Mitch was learning to read him better than anyone else ever had. That wasn't a problem, but it was getting difficult to hide things from the man. Some emotions and feelings Greg didn't confide in anyone, not even Connor.

Greg nodded and searched the storm for any sign of the machines parked right outside the cave and failed to see a single outline. "It's really gusting, the drifts will be three feet high if this keeps up." His gaze stayed riveted on the storm, half-resentful of the delay and half in awe of its power and majesty. He suddenly felt small, lonely and very isolated. The need to connect with someone seized him and he turned to Mitch.

"This is the most beautiful place on earth, even now. I remember thinking that the first time I was here. That impression's never left me. For all its power and harshness, it's still beautiful."

Mitch made a light sound somewhere between a grunt and murmur. "I remember the first time I saw you."

"You do?" Greg's eyebrows rose to his hairline.

Mitch nodded and threw another stick into the

flames. "You were standing on the landing strip, just standing there, turning around in circles, staring at the hills surrounding the air field. You looked... stunned."

"I was. Everything was too perfect." Greg stared out into the night, looking past the cloak of inky darkness and swirling snow surrounding them, remembering. "The air was clean and so crisp I could almost take a bite out of it. The blue in the sky was so bright I had to squint just to look up. And the land, the land seemed to go on forever. I've never felt anything like the rush it gave me. It was physical, like sex." He blinked and came back to the present, darting a glance at Mitch, a slight frown furrowing between his eyes. "You were there?"

"On a hill nearby." A question darkened Greg's eyes and Mitch added, "hunting."

Greg shrugged and tipped his head to one side in dismissal. "Oh. I don't remember seeing you. But I do remember looking up into the hills and seeing the most magnificent creature I've ever seen before." Greg got that far away look in his eyes again and his frown dissolved.

The expression brought a strange light to Mitch's eye and a pleased smile to his lips. He nodded and waited for the doctor to continue, as if he already knew what the man was going to say.

"I glanced around, and up in the tree line, a tiny flash of movement caught my eye. I stood as still as I could and after a few minutes, I saw him." Greg shook his head, still awed at the memory. "*The* biggest, most *gorgeous* wolf I have *ever* seen. He was awesome."

Greg moved his hands in the air like he was

actually touching the animal, stroking its fur and outlining its massive size for Mitch. "Silver gray coat so thick it must have weighed fifty pounds by itself, all puffed out and dusted with snowflakes. I could see the yellow in his eyes, even from that distance."

His eyes lit up and his face held a sense of wonder. "He was sleek and powerful and," Greg stammered and flushed, excited by his own words, "and, well, dangerous!"

He dropped his gaze, fingers tearing at a piece of kindling he had hastily picked up, his voice a low reverent tone. "You could just feel the primal energy radiating off of him. Even from that far away. I knew right then I belonged here." He glanced up at Mitch and gave him an embarrassed half grin. "This must sound stupid to you."

Mitch reached over and gently took the broken kindling from Greg's restless hands, fingers running over the other man's for just a second before he tossed the mangled stick into the fire.

"Not at all. I remember seeing a most remarkable creature for the first time that day myself, Dr. Pierce."

Laughing nervously, Greg rubbed lightly at the new knot in his stomach. He found the other man's smile exciting and mysterious. Unable to decide if Mitch was flirting with him or merely teasing him, Greg chose the saner of the two options and worked on squashing the sudden burst of interest growing in his groin.

Mitch had been his guide for over three years, since the day he arrived to start the clinic. Mitch had never shown any interest in Greg before this, at least none that Greg had detected. But Greg had to admit, he'd never really looked before.

Mitch was just… *Mitch*. Always there, always helpful, always just a comfortable part of his day, like a fresh cup of coffee or his favorite chair. A friend. A good reliable, ever present friend.

The sudden desire to share more of himself with the other man struck and before he knew it Greg was sharing another memory. He glanced quickly at Mitch to find the man watching him, a soft, unreadable expression on his face instead of the wry one he usually wore. For some reason Greg found that look comforting. He plunged ahead.

"Know why I came here? Established the clinic?" Shifting on the small campstool, Greg looked into the flames and let their flickering dance hypnotize him. Greg found it easier to talk seriously if he wasn't actually looking at anyone.

"Hunting accident." As if sensing he needed to keep his part of the conversation short, Mitch barely grunted out the answer, unwilling to stop the flow of words from the other man.

"Yep. A hunting accident." Greg closed his eyes and rubbed his hands over his face, taking a deep, fortifying breath before continuing. "It sounds so benign and trivial when you say it that way. Not at all like the life-altering, career-destroying, near-death experience it really was." He choked down a lump trying to form in the back of his throat. This was harder than he thought it would be, but Mitch was patient and quiet, waiting for Greg, as always.

Out There in the Night

"There were four of us, all avid sportsmen and experienced hunters. Came to quaint little Nekenano, Alaska on a moose-hunting trip." He shifted on the stool again and tucked his hands under his armpits to still their restless twitching.

"We went to med school together. The annual hunts were just a way to stay in touch. We were good friends, are good friends still. We all had busy lives, families, obligations, places to be, but each year we made time for this, you know?" He darted a glanced at Mitch, relieved to see the other man's face was mostly obscured by shadows. There was only a hint of yellow, a reflection from the fire, in the guide's black eyes.

Mitch sat motionless, his voice came out rough and lower pitched than usual, devoid of his usual teasing sarcasm. "You are a man who values your friends and loved ones. Though you pretend not to, all who look, can see it."

Greg squirmed on the small canvas stool and sniffed, clearing his throat twice before starting again. "Oh, well. You've got good eyes."

"Very good eyes." A wry smile tugged at the corners of Mitch's lips. "And ears, too. I can hear your heart pounding from here." The gentle sarcasm was back.

"Liar." Amused, Greg snorted, an exasperated sound.

"Believe what you want, Doc." The guide casually shrugged.

"Thanks, I will." The mood had lightened a small measure and Greg was grateful for it. "Where was I?"

Mitch threw another log on the fire to chase away the biting chill and settled back on his stool. "With friends."

"Oh, yeah. We couldn't wait to get started. Hired a guide and took off the very next morning." His eyes glazed over at the memory. "It was an absolutely fucking beautiful day."

He fell silent for so long, when Mitch spoke, it jarred him from his isolated thoughts. "What happened?"

Greg laughed, low and mirthless, blinking hard against the campfire smoke burning his eyes. "Just what we came for." A small chill ran through his body, but Greg shook it off. "The guide found a fresh trail and we tracked down our first moose. He was fabulous, a young bull with a rack so wide I could have laid in it." Greg shook his head and chewed at his upper lip.

"We'd flipped for the first shot earlier and it was Ken's win. Ken's a great guy with a terrific wife, Sherry, and three kids, all girls." Greg smiled, staring off into the darkness, and chuckled softly. "Gonna cost him a fortune in weddings in a few years."

Greg snapped back to the present and hunched closer to the fire, leaning in towards Mitch, subconsciously seeking comfort.

"Ken took his shot and the moose went down. He'd actually dropped him with one shot. It was unbelievable." Greg swallowed hard and dipped his face lower, breathing into the collar of his parka for a moment, before he raised his head, gleaming eyes blinking back sudden moisture.

"Really unbelievable. The second we got close to the thing, it reared up and bellowed like a demon breaking out of hell, kicking and bucking like… like it was fighting for its life." Greg shook his head and straightened up in his seat, his handsome face drawn and solemn. "The rest of us had been behind Ken, letting him reach the moose first, to savor the moment. You know?" He looked at Mitch for understanding and got it.

"Yes. The thrill of the kill, the victory of the hunt." Something in Mitch's voice told Greg the man knew exactly what he was describing, a deep intimate knowledge of the primal thrill of the hunt. But this time, the thrill had been empty.

"Yeah, the thrill of victory." Greg's voice sounded hollow and bitter. "Ken was too close. When the moose reared up, it nailed him with a couple of kicks before the guide managed to get off a shot and bring it down."

Greg fell silent again, trying to work his words past the lump in his throat and keep the burning wetness in his eyes from falling. It took several seconds for him to regain control. He continued the story, but avoided looking at Mitch.

"Ken's right arm, shoulder and rib cage were shattered, bones poking through the skin from every angle, blood pouring out of severed arteries, whole pieces of his flesh missing, lung punctured." Greg's chest heaved and he was panting for air. "It was a nightmare. Three experienced, top-notch surgeons at his side and we barely managed to keep him alive long enough to make it back to town." He swallowed and slowed his breathing down. "I just kept telling him once we got back, we'd get him into the nearest surgery and we'd fix everything. He'd be okay, we'd make it right." Greg straightened up on his stool and sucked in a deep, calming breathe.

"But you know what we found when we got to Nekenano?" He didn't wait for Mitch to answer. "Nothing. Absolutely nothing. Unless you count a twenty-three year old, ex-army medic with a first aid box full of outdated drugs and three rolls of gauze."

"How did you keep him alive?" Mitch murmured.

"We gave him transfusions directly from Rob. They share the same blood type. Got a supply plane diverted to us and got him to Anchorage. He was in surgery for over eighteen hours." Greg stared into the fire and sniffed, self-consciously wiping at his face. "Ken lived, but let's face it, there isn't much call for a one-armed brain surgeon."

Surprised, Mitch asked, "He blames you for his loss?"

"What? Hell no!" Greg darted an astonished glance at Mitch. "Ken was grateful to be alive. He understood how limited we were. And Sherry... Sherry was just thrilled to have him back." He sniffed again and wiped his thumb over the corner of one eye. "They're the ones who gave me that green scarf I always wear. A replacement for the one I ruined that day using it as a tourniquet. The one Connor took."

"Ah, yes." Mitch leaned back and frowned at Greg. "The cloak of guilt you wear so faithfully."

Mitch's accusing proclamation struck a direct hit

on Greg's heart. He flushed and bristled, "What the hell do you know about it?"

Mitch shrugged again. "I know when a man is driven by strong emotions. Even in your constant quest to hide your true self, the caring soul of a healer leaks out. The spirits talk of it." He cocked his head and winked conspiratorially at Greg. "Your secrets are known to those who take the time to listen."

In his heart, Greg knew the man was right. The scarf *was* his constant reminder of his responsibility and obligation to the clinic and the people of his adopted town. His anger sputtered out, replaced with exhaustion and worry.

Greg sighed and managed a small smile. "Those good ears of yours again, huh?"

"Among other things, yes." Mitch nodded and a smile lit up his dark eyes.

"Well, you're right about one thing. The frustration, the sheer *helplessness*," Greg pounded his fists on his knees, the words forced out between gritted teeth, "all right, *the guilt*, of knowing what to do to save Ken, but almost failing, nearly killed me." He stared at his hands, hands that had saved hundreds of lives and restored hope to thousands of patients, but couldn't save the arm of his best friend.

Greg ran both hands through his hair, and then over his face, trying to wipe away the memory and his emotions. "I came back and opened the clinic as soon as I could get all the elements in place for it." He kicked at an ember that rolled out of the fire, sending it back into the flames. "It's a struggle to keep it staffed with qualified doctors, but inheriting a mountain of money to work with helps."

"Doctors like yourself and Dr. Jacy." Mitch mused softly. "He is a kind man and a good healer."

"Yeah, like Connor." Greg searched the blackness outside the dim ring of firelight, unable to see more than a few feet away. Fear touched his eyes and he turned back to Mitch. "I just hope we don't find him in the kind of shape we found Dark. It's a hell of a long way back to town this time."

Mitch laid a comforting hand on Greg's shoulder. "But there is now a clinic to go to. Because of you."

"Yeah, because of me." Bitterness dripped from his words and twisted his face. Worry and self-loathing settled into his eyes. "All of this is because of me."

Mitch grunted and tossed another log into the flames. "No, Doctor Pierce. Not unless you're responsible for marauding wolves or Justin Loken's wife getting pregnant."

Greg gave a startled grunt of surprise.

Mitch paused for a moment looking as if he was trying to fight back a grin. He cast an amused, assessing glance over Greg and added, "Both of which I doubt."

Whether it was the comic glance from the corner of his eye, or the sarcastic, knowing tone of Mitch's voice, Greg chuckled. "You're right, as usual. I'm innocent on both counts." He heaved a deep, defeated sigh. "It just... doesn't feel like it."

Mitch accepted the confession in silence.

Two of the other members of the search party rolled from their sleeping bags and stood up, preparing to relieve them.

Mitch stretched and gestured toward the back of the cave. "Come. It is time for sleep. The storm will pass when the winds decide and not until." He stood and waited for Greg to follow him.

Tired but anxious, Greg waved him off. "I'm not tired yet." When Mitch didn't move, Greg glanced up him, then away, stubbornly focusing on the fire.

Mitch wasn't so easily sidetracked. He laid a hand on Greg's shoulder and squeezed it firmly. "Just rest then. There may be many sleepless nights ahead when your strength will be required for others to draw on."

Understanding the unspoken warning he might be faced with another all-night bedside vigil after hours of grueling surgery, Greg gave a weary sigh and stood. He let Mitch lead the way to their bedrolls and reluctantly settled in. The stress and the exhaustion of the last two days crept up quickly on Greg. He was softly snoring before Mitch had even settled down beside him.

***

Chapter Eight

It had been four days since the accident, but Connor's heavy-lidded gaze was still out of focus. His eyes followed Adam's bare-chested figure as he walked slowly around the small cabin filling smudge pots with a dried mixture Connor didn't recognize. Adam carefully lit each pot with a thin sliver of kindling from the crackling fire, the only source of light in the shadow-filled room. A thin ribbon of brown smoke drifted up from each clay pot lacing the air with a faintly sweet scent. Adam passed by Connor, depositing a small, red clay pot filled with what appeared to be a kind of dark lard on the square table beside the bed.

Before long, Connor's head felt stuffy and his vision blurred even more, but the constant pounding behind his eyes dulled. A light euphoric feeling began to seep into his body. He forced himself to focus on Adam's face, trying to ignore the way the defined muscles on the man's chest and abdomen rippled, then flowed out to blur at the edges of his body. Dancing firelight glistened on the sweaty surface of the big man's skin mesmerizing Connor before his medical training and simple common sense kicked in. He sniffed the air, wrinkling his nose.

"What is that? Some kind of Alaskan peyote?"

The room was becoming overly warm and Connor pushed at the quilt, shoving it down to his waist, mindless of his nude state hiding under its protective covering.

Kneeling by the hearth to work the flames to a higher pitch, Adam smiled and tossed the burnt kindling piece into the fire.

"No. My people call it *'iqemik'*. It is a local mushroom. The ashes are normally rolled with tobacco and smoked in a pipe or chewed." He rose effortlessly from the floor and dusted off his knees, firelight forming a halo around his torso. "It has many uses." A small grin tugged the corners of his full mouth wider. "Medicinal and otherwise." Back facing the fire, Adam's dark eyes somehow caught in the reflected firelight and they glowed a rusty orange.

Connor blinked hard to wash away the illusion, but Adam just seemed to grow larger and his smooth skin turned dark and fur-covered. After a few blinks, Adam returned to his usual indistinct, but god-like image for Connor. Connor frowned. "I think my eyes are playing tricks on me again. You looked... furry for a minute there."

"Your head injury was great. It will take time for you to heal." Voice tender and roughened by emotion, Adam walked closer to the bed. "Until then, I will care for you, Connor."

Unable to think of a suitable answer that wouldn't reveal his heart too soon, Connor ignored the statement and concentrated on watching Adam move, continuing to be enthralled by the big man's sinewy grace and raw power.

Turning to face Connor fully, Adam let his eyes wander over the doctor's disheveled blond hair down to the partially discarded quilt, his gaze lingering over every inch of the newly exposed flesh on the lean, smoothly muscled chest. A trail of pale, fine hair formed a V-shape across Connor's puckered nipples, tapering down to disappear under the covers. Connor felt as if Adam's sharp gaze didn't miss a single follicle.

Stomach contracting in excitement, Connor swallowed hard and let his own gaze drop to follow Adam's large, callused hands as they began to unlace the ties to his pants.

The butter-soft hide pants slid silently over Adam's thickly muscled hips and buttocks, gliding to the floor in a puddle of gold. He stepped out of them, leaving his moccasins behind as well, and walked to the edge of the bed.

Connor instinctively moved to the center of the bed to make room, lifting the quilt in a mute invitation for Adam to join him under the covers alongside his naked and very willing body.

The sight of Adam's erect, uncircumcised cock grabbed Connor's full attention. The deep bronze shaft was long, and hooded by a dark cap of taut foreskin. Its veined length was topped with a large head that flowed down to an unusually thick, bulbous base nestled in a forest of black hair so thick it looked like an animal pelt. Connor had the urge to reach out and pet it, just to know if it was as soft as it appeared.

Excitement burned in his groin and his cock responded by growing harder. Connor inhaled deeply to regain control and the room spun as the sweet odor from the smudge pots filled his head. Outside the raging winds dulled to a low roar, while the crackle and spit of the fire seemed unnaturally loud and crisp to him.

"Room's warm." He pulled his gaze from Adam's groin and glanced up self-consciously, licking his dry lips. "Doesn't it feel warm to you?"

The offer of the open quilt was still there and Adam slid onto the bed, taking the cover from Connor's unresisting hand.

"It is warm. I wanted you to be comfortable."

"I am comfortable." Connor gasped as Adam's hard, chiseled chest pressed against his side. "Just, you know," he swallowed hard again, "...warm." As the ends of Adam's long hair teased his chest, a shiver ghosted through his body, contradicting his words.

Adam tugged on the quilt and Connor released it, a look of dismay breaking over his face as it was whisked to the floor to join the discarded pants, leaving him naked and exposed to the heavy, warm air of the cabin.

"Comfortable, without that," Adam murmured. He ran a hand lightly over Connor's chest then dragged the back of his fingers down to circle his belly button. Smiling at Connor's sudden, sharp intake of air, he added, "I can not worship what I can not see."

Connor gave a little huffed, nervous laugh. "Worship? Me?" His self-conscious gaze turned smoldering under heavy eyelids, his eyes drawn to the sensuous curve of Adam's biceps and broad shoulders.

"There's only one god-like creature in this room and it sure as hell isn't me." Growing bolder, he traced his fingertips down the valley of Adam's sternum.

At the tentative first touch from the shy young man, Adam leaned over, encircling Connor in his arms.

105

Lips barely inches apart, he stroked his fingers down the side of Connor's face and whispered into his parted, now panting mouth.

"Then it is well my people do not worship gods."

He closed the gap between them; lips sealed together in a searing kiss that made Connor's stomach flutter in response. Adam pulled back slightly and continued talking, his deep voice, his formal words hypnotic and soothing as he rained feather-light kisses over Connor's upturned face.

"We value the spirit that lies within a person's soul." He placed a breathy ghost of a kiss on each of Connor's closed eyelids. There was a touch of teasing humor in his sultry voice when he added, "But that does not mean we cannot worship the vessel the spirit is stored in."

Adam kissed his way down Connor's face, exploring every sensitive landmark on the lean, lithe body.

Connor squirmed and panted with each wet, teasing swirl of tongue that invaded the outer shell of his ear, and traced the arch of his neck. He shivered with every nip of even, sharp, white teeth that marked the line of his jaw, and gasped aloud when his nipples were voraciously tasted, their crinkled buds firmly suckled and teased into fiery peaks of aching flesh. Little shocks of electric pleasure exploded in his chest. Needing something to anchor the wildly spiraling sensations, he wove his fingers deep into Adam's hair, tangling them in the midnight black veil of silk.

Drawing a deep breath to steady himself only

caused the room to spin. The scent of the ash became stronger and it gathered at the back of his throat adding a sweet taste to his mouth. The silky hair in his hands suddenly seemed to grow thicker and Adam's weight magnified as he leaned against Connor.

Arching his back, Connor pressed his chest more tightly to Adam and opened his eyes, determined to watch his new lover suckle at his tit. In a brief flash of blurry, lust-induced fantasy, a pair of rusty-orange eyes glowing from a feral face surrounded by rich, black fur replaced Adam's face.

Blinking hard, Connor jerked as a sharp nip grazed his burning nipple and the vision dissolved, leaving only the broad-boned, smooth face of his increasingly dominant, sensual lover.

As if sensing Connor's unease, Adam broke away. Planting a lick on each reddened bud, he moved up to thoroughly kiss him, sliding his very talented tongue so deeply into Connor's mouth he felt it touch the back of his soft palate.

For a moment Connor imagined it to be like the tongue of a panting wolf, long and meaty, curling to lap and taste his mouth. Panicked, he reached up and lightly traced Adam's high cheek bones and square, hairless jaw to reassure himself it was all just an illusion, a side effect of the ash and his concussion. Satisfied when his hands met smooth, sweaty flesh, he sighed and allowed Adam to deepen the possessive kiss.

From now on, if he had fantasies of Adam as a huge, gorgeous, feral beast, he was just going to go with them. After all, they weren't real and he had to admit it, that tongue was one talented muscle.

The sudden erotic image of Adam's tongue deep in his ass formed in his mind and his asshole fluttered and spasmed. His fully erect cock jerked, excited by the idea. A warm, callused hand wrapped around it, firmly holding him by the shaft. Connor hissed as Adam pulled away to rise up onto his knees.

Adam splayed Connor's legs apart, pulling them over his own thighs so he could position himself between them. He sat back on his heels, still keeping a firm grip on Connor's cock, his hand slowly sweeping up and down the slender, pink shaft. Oddly, Adam's gaze wandered around the room before his heated stare settled back on Connor's face.

"The spiritwalkers have come. They will witness and bless this union tonight." Reaching for the red clay pot on the side table, Adam released his hold on Connor. "First we must open the pathway to your soul so our spirits may bond."

"Spirits?" Connor popped his head up, eyes darting around looking into the shadowed corners of the dimly lit room, seeing nothing but the same crude furniture and sparse trappings as before.

Staring up at Adam, he carefully lowered his spinning head back down onto the pillow. "Bonded? Adam, I don't think --." Adam's quiet conviction alarmed him.

"You do not have to think, Connor. Our path is already set. You just have to follow."

Adam scooped out a large portion of the thick greasy substance from the clay pot and began rubbing it over his own chest. It left a heavy film of dark red dust on his skin, so dark it looked as if he had been painted in old blood from his neck to his waist.

Connor closed his eyes and willed away the slight dizziness the sudden movement of his head had caused. He was unnerved by the nagging, conscious knowledge he was losing the will to resist Adam. He opened his eyes and found himself enthralled by the sweeping motion of Adam's strong, wide hands as they rubbed layer after layer of rusty red dust over Adam's flexing torso. Unable to unlock his gaze from the hypnotic ritual, Connor did manage to force out a half-hearted protest.

"You're talking about a lifetime commitment. You don't even know me."

Adam began stroking his hands up and down the sides of his torso, letting each deep breath ripple the muscles of his body in a slow steady rhythm.

Connor found it all highly erotic and seductive. He bit his lower lip to help him focus and tried again. "I-I barely know you."

Tossing the pot onto the far side of the bed, Adam crouched atop Connor. Cradled snuggly between the doctor's legs, he planted his stout arms on either side of Connor's slim shoulders and stared into Connor's green eyes.

"I know all I need to know about you, Connor Jacy. My heart is already yours and soon all that I am will be revealed to you -- my true spirit, my soul."

He lowered himself down onto Connor's body. The silver bands braided into Adam's long hair sparkled, his thick locks glistening blue-black in the firelight. The ends swung free, brushing over Connor's skin, making his flesh tingle.

Pressing chest to chest again, Adam propped himself up on his elbows and fingered Connor's light blond hair. His tone was awestruck and reverent.

"The fire makes your hair turn to threads of gold and silver. Moonlight will do the same." Adam played with the strands as he whispered, his pleading, dark eyes locked on Connor's confused ones.

"Before the time of revelation comes to pass, I must be in your heart." Adam placed both of his clay-stained hands on Connor's face and slowly massaged the red dust into his pale skin, working his way over whatever skin he could touch.

"What are you doing?" Growing breathless, Connor could feel the fine powder ingraining itself into his every pore, soft and silky like fine cornstarch. "What is this stuff?"

Even as he asked, Connor knew he didn't really care. The powerful hands felt good roaming over his body and his cock had long ago lost interest in the 'whys' of the situation.

Rubbing down each of Connor's lean arms, Adam's touch was sensual and arousing, coaxing out Connor's primal, lustful nature that was buried under his modern-day cloak of medical science and reasoning.

"The dust symbolizes the blood of my ancestors now dwelling in the spirit world. It opens a path for my soul." He flexed his torso, again rubbing his chest over Connor's, marking the smaller man's entire upper half in red. "Every grain of dust that marks your flesh from mine is a pathway for our spirits to meet."

He nuzzled Connor's neck and panted heavily in

his ear, hips slowly grinding down to rub their cocks together.

"It marks a place where my spirit may enter you, to join with you, to open the path for our bodies to join as well."

He bit down the arch of Connor's neck, forcing a strangled gasp out of him. "Join with me, Connor. Trust me. Let me in."

Adam's hands and chest were suddenly everywhere. Rubbing, grinding, soothing, and petting until Connor was nearly wild with aching need. Eyes clenched tight, every inch of his skin sizzled as the rough, callused hands worked him over. His nipples burned, his engorged cock pulsed with the rapid pounding of his heart, his opening spasmed between tightly clenched butt cheeks and even his mouth felt swollen, all hungry for attention.

His hips were raised in the air, allowing Adam to drag Connor's open crotch over his chest. The feeling of the soft silky powder coating his most sensitive areas made Connor gasp. He bucked against the hard chest and gave a strangled grunt when his cock was suddenly sucked into a steaming hot vortex and surrounded by a tight, wet muscle.

Supported by his shoulders, his hips in Adam's large, strong arms, his bent legs over broad shoulders, Connor watched as Adam devoured his cock, licking and sucking down the shaft to the base with ease. His entire body shook with delight when a deep low growl rumbled through Adam's chest. The sound vibrated through his cock and shot up his spine, ending in a burst of white light behind his eyes.

Adam shifted his hold slightly and Connor could feel a blunt pressure at the entrance to his body. Just as he was about to object, the pressure became a sensual stroking and his own body answered the questing exploration by fluttering around the broad fingertip. It lodged at the welcoming opening, entering only to the point where Connor was conscious of its presence. It slowly began a circular rubbing, loosening and teasing the tight band of muscle until Connor had to fight down the urge to thrust down and impale himself on it.

The smell of the ash teased his nose and the crackle and pop of the fire became muted in the background. A soft, barely-there chanting in a language he understood but shouldn't have, filled the air. He opened his eyes to take in the sight of his powerful new lover and lust rocketed through him. He watched as the cinnamon-bronze beast between his legs mouthed and tugged at his balls, then lapped a long, supple tongue around the base of his straining cock.

Connor locked gazes with Adam, causing his lover to leave his sac and move up to deep-throat his cock. He bucked and hissed as his shaft was sucked hard, a thick meaty tongue swirling around the leaking head in a dance of lust that made him see stars.

New sensations of want and need were stirring from deep inside him. He felt helpless to resist -- didn't want to, couldn't think how to.

Connor rode the wild tide of desire Adam had created, giving his quietly dominant lover total control. Like the alpha wolf Connor kept envisioning in Adam, his lover made it clear he would have nothing but total submission from Connor tonight. For the first time in his life, Connor would give everything he had.

On the brink of climax, Connor nearly screamed when the delicious hot tongue and mouth disappeared and the cooler air of the cabin struck his wet, aching cock.

Catching his breath, he let Adam's powerful arms turn him over and shove a pillow under his hips. As he was settled down onto the feather-filled case, a callused hand snaked under him and pulled his cock down, positioning it between his parted thighs. A satiny smooth weight descended on his back and roughened, gentle hands rubbed and kneaded his skin as a hard chest pressed over every inch of Connor's heated arms and back.

A moist, panting whisper tickled his ear and Connor strained to understand the low, growled words.

"With each marking we are bonded for life, Connor Jacy. Tonight we join, spirit, mind and body. Tonight, we become like creatures, skinwalkers, mated for all time, eternal and true."

"I don't understand. Adam?"

Connor turned his head on the pillow and looked over his shoulder to catch a glimpse of Adam's face. A wide, heavy hand pushed him back onto the mattress and stayed there, rubbing a small circle between his shoulder blades as if to apologize for pinning him in place.

"Trust me," was whispered in his ear in a guttural groan that sounded more animal growl than human voice.

Surrendering, Connor stared across the room at

the blazing hearth, drawing comfort from the familiar, cheery sight of the flames. A slight movement caught his eye and he stared, mesmerized and fascinated as the shadows around the edges of the room began to sway and dance, taking on human forms dressed in native garb. The faint chanting already in the air became more distinct.

Connor blinked and rubbed a hand over his eyes to wipe away the vision, noticing as he did, his entire arm, hand and each finger were a dark red.

The figures never faded, but neither did they come closer, staying at the edges of the darkened cabin. Connor fingered the suture line on his forehead, wondering just how much damage his brain actually had suffered with the concussion.

A deep growl of desire from Adam vibrated through his back. He felt Adam's weight increase then lift slightly as the big man slid down, rubbing his dust-layered chest over Connor's back and buttocks. Fevered hands stroked and caressed up and down his spread legs, each touch like a branding iron on Connor's over-sensitive skin.

Strong fingers kneaded his ass. He felt his butt cheeks pulled apart, a pair of roughly callused thumbs sweeping circles over his ready hole in a tantalizing rhythm that sent sparks of pleasure straight to the center of his groin.

"Christ! Adam!"

Connor groaned and jerked with each pass of the sandpaper-like tips, his ass desperate for some type of heavier stimulation. As a gay man who had spent his entire sexual life avoiding anal penetration, he was stunned at how much his body was craving it, demanding it, begging for it.

Just when he thought he couldn't stand another pass of the sensual caress, the dry, hot rubbing and warm puffs of breath were replaced with an even more intense sensation.

"Fuck!"

Connor literally jumped and grunted when Adam's wet, thick tongue licked up his trapped shaft, over his tight sac and stretched flesh to finally lap hungrily at the clenched rim of his opening. After a few broad-tongued strokes, the slick intrusion turned to an insistent jabbing motion that made Connor ache for more.

Muted snuffling sounds floated up from his backside and Connor pressed back against the muscle invading his loosening channel. All of his senses seemed magnified and out of focus. Connor panted into the pillow, clenching his fists in the dust-stained sheets.

Trying to concentrate on the heart-stopping pleasure Adam was giving him, he closed his eyes to block out the rest of the mystical visions in the room. He tried to add a mental picture to the sensations in his ass. He felt a patch of cool wetness at the top of the cleft of his cheeks, a fine rub of soft bristles along his crack and a tantalizing scratch and nibble on the flesh of his cheeks.

The stiff, jabbing tongue slid impossibly deep into him, caressing the tingling nerve ending just beyond the once-tight opening to his body. Every lick and wiggle inside forced a low moan from Connor and soon he was thrusting his hips into the pillow, instinctively seeking stimulation for his neglected cock.

On the third thrust, his hips were seized and his body was forced back and up onto his hands and knees. Adam's tongue was still buried deeply in his hole, busily tormenting the kernel of soft, spongy tissue it had found with the change of position.

Connor's face contorted into a grimace at the added stimulation of his prostate. He hissed and wailed out a plea. "Christ Almighty! Adam, do something, please, before my head blows off."

Connor shook his head from side to side, spraying droplets of sweat onto the bed from his chin and the ends of his disheveled blond hair. "Touch me. Do anything! Just make me cum. Please!"

A warm, satiny soft cloak descended on his back. Before his body registered the change in Adam's position, a wide, blunt heat replaced the tongue at the entrance to his body. A lock of thick, black hair fell across his shoulder and down into his face, while his neck and hair were nuzzled and bitten. Adam's voice was unusually deep in his ear, a sensual growl of sultry desire. He could smell himself on Adam's breath as the man whispered into his neck.

"Not yet, adada, but soon, very soon. Just trust me."

Connor's protest died on his lips as Adam lunged forward and impaled the smaller man onto his cock in one powerful thrust. Instead of the searing pain and nausea he had expected, Connor experienced a storm of electric sensation that stole his breath away.

The room swam and his head pounded in time

to the long, deep strokes in his ass. He could feel the thick ridges that ran the length of Adam's shaft rippling against the tight channel. The ample foreskin he dreamed about tasting bunched into a thick ring on each forward stroke, creating a knot of pressure against untouched nerves lining his passageway. The huge knob on the tip of Adam's cock rubbed unerringly over his prostate with each backward stroke.

Connor felt his orgasm building. His balls slapped the furry pelt growing over Adam's entire groin and down his strong thighs in an increasingly rapid rhythm. Unable to turn his head to see his lover, Connor gasped out a warning of his approaching climax.

"Fuck, man, you got me, Adam, you got me!"

His panted words were met with a quickening of deeper thrusts from behind and a hot, burning stream of wetness flooded his ass.

From behind him, Adam growled and grunted, jerking Connor back roughly to hold him motionless against his groin, pulsing cock embedded to the root.

The nerves at Connor's opening burned at being forced so wide so suddenly. Sizzling, white-hot pain/pleasure flooded his senses, traveling up his spine to his thoroughly dazed brain triggering his climax. His cock erupted, splattering his chest and arms with a long, thin rope of cum.

Strong hands bluntly kneaded his bruised hips, but didn't release their iron grip. The peak of his climax faded and Connor basked in the curiously hypersensitive feeling enfolding him. If this was standard anal intercourse, he was sorry he had missed out on it all these years. But something told him it would only be like this if Adam was the one loving him.

Connor wanted to fall on the bed in a heap of sated exhaustion, but Adam's hold wouldn't let him. He pushed back tentatively at the man and turned his head to look over his shoulder, but was immediately stopped by a hand in his hair gently holding him still. Connor didn't resist, but called out softly to his forceful lover.

"Adam? Talk to me?"

The hand rubbed through his hair then released him. Adam's deep, rumbling tones soothed Connor's unease. "This is not a time for words, adada."

Something rubbed over a patch of skin between Connor's shoulder blades leaving the flesh feeling abraded as if coarse sandpaper had been used.

"It is the time for only our hearts to speak." Adam's voice was indistinct and his words were marked with a lisp, like someone talking around a new set of braces, but the sincerity and love in it were clear.

Connor let his head drop and he relaxed back against the tower of stout flesh impaling him. "All right. Let our hearts talk then." Despite knowing Adam had cum, Connor could tell the man hadn't slipped out or even diminished in size.

Sensation began to creep back into Connor's body and he became aware of a growing pressure just past the rim of stretched muscle inside his ass. The intense pressure reawakened the barely recovered nerves. Connor began to pant at the growing sensation, like he was coaching a first time mother through childbirth. The pressure reached a level of discomfort

Connor could barely tolerate then stopped.

Connor pulled forward, intending to slip off Adam's shaft a few inches to ease the fullness in his passageway. He found it impossible to do. He couldn't pull free and each attempt to do so merely increased the buzz and tingle of fullness in his ass. Suddenly the world seemed to center around the pleasure radiating from his stuffed channel.

Spiraling into a dream world of indescribable pleasure, delirious with sensation and the euphoric aftermath of an explosive orgasm, Connor sensed a change in the room. The insistent chanting grew marginally softer and the shadows around the room retreated back near the walls. Even the smell of the burning ash turned sweeter and the sounds outside the cabin disappeared entirely.

One of Adam's arms dropped down for support, his fist landing next to Connor's as he leaned over, cradling Connor with his broad body. Changing his thrusts, Adam began snapping his hips in a rapid-fire staccato rhythm, jabbing his swollen cock deeply into Connor's most hidden recesses.

The hammering motion jarred Connor's entire body and each stroke, both forward and back, pounded the engorged base of Adam's cock against the clenched ring of nerves and muscles locking them together like dogs in heat. The effect was wildly overwhelming and Connor threw back his head and screamed.

"Ah! God, God, God! Jesus!"

Fire raced through every cell of his body. He felt like even his hair would burst into flame. The thick, viscous cum Adam had emptied into his ass only a moment ago coated his channel, dripping into the folds and lessening the friction the frenzied thrusts were generating. Connor burned inside and out, every pore seeming to leak heat along with his sweat.

Tossing his head to one side to push a clump of sweat-soaked, clinging hair from his eyes, Connor looked down and absently noted Adam's straining, cinnamon-stained arm was now covered in black fur. The fist Adam supported his weight on was now a massive canine paw. When Connor turned his face as far as it would go over his shoulder, a dark muzzle entered the edge of his vision.

Undisturbed by the now-familiar hallucinations, Connor closed his eyes and listened to his heart, letting every sensation he was experiencing seep into his awareness, reveling in each and every one of them.

The pelt of hair pressing against his butt cheeks remained soft, but the entrance to his ass prickled, abraded by fine bristles of stiff hair. The hot breath on his back came in pants, a soft whine underlying the labored breaths. The teeth nibbling his neck were sharp and long, leaving streaks of broken skin in their wake. The powerful thighs hammering against his legs bulged impossibly large and hard, yet felt silky, like down, where their inner creases smacked his wildly swaying scrotum. All the sensations merged together as another burning blast of cum washed over Connor's insides.

Distracted by his visions, Connor nearly missed his own building orgasm. He bucked and screamed as a massive, nearly painful climax exploded from deep within his balls. It tore up his cock and dribbled a small offering onto the sheets.

Out There in the Night

Connor's arms suddenly turned into limp, useless supports that collapsed under his own weight. As he fell, Connor felt his hips and torso pulled close and gently turned. He landed on his back, still impaled on Adam's unrelenting erection. His limbs were tenderly gathered closer to his sweat-drenched body.

Resting on his knees, Adam settled Connor's ass close to his groin to minimize the tugging pressure locking them together. He folded Connor's unresisting legs up toward the man's heaving chest, grabbing them by the ankles. Connor's knees relaxed outward, exposing his flaccid cock and spent sac.

Looking down at his dust-encrusted body, Connor was hard-pressed to see a single patch of pale skin through the dark clay. Laughing softly, he gestured at his open groin.

"If you're looking for any spots you missed, I think you got *that* part covered, big guy. It's been blessed as much as it can take. I surrender." He cupped his spent cock, stroking it, showing Adam the visible lack of response.

Chuckling, Adam smiled mysteriously and gently thrust his hips forward. Connor's ass fluttered around the fat shaft and his senses flared. He moaned and bucked against the sudden shift in pressure. Nerve endings sizzled and his flaccid cock jumped, instantly filling to half-mast.

Connor palmed the hardening shaft once before letting it fall from his hand, groaning up at Adam. "You're killing me."

"No one's ever died from making love, Connor. You won't be the first." Adam flexed his hips again.

121

Connor hissed and pressed his ass deeper onto Adam's lap, sparking a new round of burning sensation inside his ass.

Pulling Connor's legs up higher, Adam placed the soles of Connor's feet on his red-stained chest, just over his heart. He slowly rubbed them through the remains of the clay dust, coating them in red.

"This is the final path for my spirit into your body, Connor. Now our souls are forever entwined. One will not be complete without the other from this day onward." Adam lifted each foot in turn, massaging the dust into the skin then lowering it to the bed. "Now, your footsteps will forever follow my path. Your spirit will always know the way to my lodge. Your heart will dwell in mine. We are one."

Adam pulled Connor more tightly to him and began a slow, sensual thrusting, a minute movement of his powerful hips. The gentle rocking motion awakened all of Connor's senses and his body began to respond in earnest once more. Connor shook and panted, instinctively wrapping his legs around Adam's waist. He felt fully dominated and claimed by this exotic warrior, in both body and soul.

Connor could feel the hot, blunt tip of the thick shaft pulsing in his abdomen, just below his belly button, creating friction against the smooth sides of his tightly stretched channel. The erotically charged, hugely intimate position brought a sudden flash of nervousness to Connor's chest.

This mysterious, quietly dominating, possessive, god-like man had been a complete stranger only a few days ago. Now, with his cock still buried deep in

Connor's body, Adam talked of merged spirits, common paths and eternity together. Connor knew his world changed with each new thrust of Adam's cock.

The chanting in the background became louder, and for the first time, he could hear the beat of drums. The rhythm swelled and an immense burst of molten lava-like heat seemed to flow out of Adam's cock into Connor's ass. It coursed through his body, burning everything it touched, leaving behind a crushing heaviness that made it hard for Connor to breathe.

Frantic, Connor grabbed at Adam. Finding Adam's thick-fingered hands gripping his hips, he laced their fingers tightly together.

Adam moved down to rest on Connor's chest. What little air remained in Connor's lungs rushed out in a deep grunt. His breathing was challenged yet again as his lover sealed their mouths together and sucked the air from his body along with his tongue.

The slow thrusts remained unchanged in rhythm, but Adam began to build up the force behind them. Each stroke rocked Connor hard enough to shove him up the bed until he eventually met the headboard.

Rather than move back down the bed, Adam grabbed onto the rough planks of the headboard and used them to increase his thrusts.

The air in the small cabin grew heavy and everywhere Connor looked a shadow danced and chanted. A deep, throaty wolf howl had started outside, its haunting sound carried on the winds and repeated by a new voice every few minutes. Connor turned away from his blurring visions to gaze up at Adam.

The dark, cinnamon-bronze of Adam's natural complexion was enhanced by a fine sheen of sweat on his skin, its wetness capturing the firelight and accenting his sharp-edged, broad bone structure. His hard-muscled body and sinewy limbs flexed and strained, powerful and overwhelmingly erotic in their graceful strength. The full satin cloak of his black hair flowed around the two of them like a veil of protection, blocking outsiders from their intimate world of unleashed passion. Behind the lust and the desire in the deep, wide-set black eyes, Connor saw what he had been looking for all his life -- profound love and acceptance. The searing leaden feeling suddenly melted from his body like a spring thaw and he felt a rush of primal energy race through him, filling the void.

Reaching up, he pulled Adam back down into a heated kiss, taking time to explore and to taste, heedless of his own need to breathe. The jarring thrusts increased to a frenzied paced until both men cried out, their voices merging as one, as their bodies spilled their passions.

Exhausted beyond description, Connor was only faintly aware of Adam turning him onto his side and wrapping his arms around him. His opening spasmed with the movement, reminding him Adam was still buried inside. The thought that Adam would always be inside of him, whether they were coupling or not, flashed across his mind and burrowed into the center of his heart.

He hissed and moaned at the tugging sensation in his ass as Adam wiggled closer and plastered his body to Connor's back. A warm hand smoothed the bedraggled hair from his face and puffs of air filled with the smell of burnt ash teased his exposed ear. Adam's voice came to him through a fog, rich and soothing.

"Sleep, adada. It will take some time before my body releases you." A light kiss landed on Connor's neck and trailed up to his ear where Adam added, "But know that my heart never will."

Connor tried to answer, tried to make his lips form words of acceptance and mutual promise, but his mind couldn't respond. He only managed a sigh of contentment before awareness slipped away and the shadow dancers came for him.

***

Chapter Nine

Morning came and went, but the unexpected storm continued to batter the hillside where the tiny cave stood with its restless inhabitants. On the second day, the sky cleared and the snow stopped, but the winds still raged. The day was bright and crisp. The snow so white it sparkled like diamonds, distorting a person's vision if they stared at it too long.

Despite the winds, the ten-man team hurriedly set off again, heading for Raven Gully, the last known place Connor had been seen.

The trail was difficult to travel, obliterated by the blowing snow. It was uneven and deep, often requiring them to form a single line and maneuver slowly around fissures and hidden rocks. The winds whipped at them, snagging caps and goggles, seemingly fighting them every inch of the way.

Greg noticed only Mitch seemed unfazed by the fierce gale. The guide steadfastly led them through the dangerous passageways, weathered face turned into the stormy winds. Greg marveled at the man's skill and fortitude. A few miles out, Greg began to notice the way Mitch occasionally cocked his head to one side and nodded, as if he was listening to the turbulent howling conversing with him.

By late afternoon the men finally arrived at the gully, tired but elated to have made some headway in the search for the missing young doctor. Tucked away in a secluded, naturally protected ravine, they found the evidence of the accident that was still visible.

Mitch silenced his snow machine and walked to a dark stain on the snow near several deep ruts in the icy ground. The other men fanned out around the perimeter of the accident scene, experienced enough at the job to know not to disturb things until Mitch or Joss had examined them first. Every clue here would be important if they were going to find Connor.

Aware of Mitch's need to be allowed to have time to explore the site, but anxious to know something concrete, Greg edged closer to his guide. He remained out of the way, but shuffled his feet and loudly clapped his hands together to warm them, a gesture he knew annoyed Mitch and never failed to get his attention.

Within seconds, Mitch shot him a mild glare over his shoulder. Greg froze, then idly stuffed his hands into his pockets and began whistling softly under his breath. But not so softly Mitch couldn't hear him.

The guide sighed and gave up. He crouched down and pointed at depressions and multiple, large, dark stains in the snow at his feet. "This is where Dark went down. Right next to the sled. He took a lot of the sled's weight in the fall." He ran a hand along a deep dent in the hard-packed snow. "His leg must have gotten trapped by it at some point, too."

Greg nodded and stepped closer, relieved when Mitch didn't glare at him again. "Probably how he broke his ribs and arm. It wasn't the wolf, he didn't have a bite mark on him."

"But there were wolves here." Mitch brushed a glove over the animal tracks in the snow. "Wolf prints. Here," he pointed to the left then to the right, "and here.

Large ones."

Mitch stood and followed the animal tracks until they led to another stain in the snow several yards away. As he approached the stain, a colorful, fluttering motion in a leafless bush to his left caught his attention. He bent down and pulled a green strip off the twig where it was snagged. He turned back and gestured to Greg to come to him, then silently handed over his find.

Greg took it, immediately recognizing it as a piece of his scarf that Connor had been wearing. It was tattered, the fibers shredded, as if powerful, sharp teeth or claws had torn it. It was also spotted with dark smudges.

Not wanting to know the truth, but unable to stop, Greg rubbed one of the stains and brought the fabric to his nose to sniff it. The unmistakable odor of old blood hit him and his stomach rolled, not because of the scent, but because of what it meant for Connor.

The last time Greg had seen this scarf, it had been tightly wrapped around the young man's neck and buried under his coat collar. It would have taken a lot to be torn off his body and destroyed in such a vicious manner.

Greg looked at Mitch and found the guide patiently waiting for a response from him. He knew Mitch understood what this meant even more than he did. As a hunter and tracker, there wasn't much Mitch hadn't seen in his day, including the aftermath of a wolf pack feasting on downed prey.

"What else do you see, Mitch?" Greg jutted his chin in the direction of the large dark stain in the packed ground beneath the bush. Falling back on his detached, professional training, Greg managed to keep his voice steady and firm. "Doesn't look like there's as much blood here."

"There is less." Mitch ran his hand over the small, bowl-shaped depression in the ice hard snow, pointing out how it lay in the middle of the stain. Plucking a strand of bloodstained hair from the ice, he handed the fine blond strand to Greg. "Looks like Dr. Jacy hit his head, hard, right here."

Wordlessly Greg accepted the grisly find, but a gust of wind tore it from his gloved fingers and it disappeared into the growing twilight. Greg followed it with his eyes for a moment, then turned to give Mitch a grim nod.

"Find him, Mitch. I'm depending on you."

A gust of wind swirled around them and Mitch cocked his head slightly. Greg had the definite impression the guide was listening to the winds again.

Mitch pulled in a deep breath and let his gaze wander around the hillside before he spoke. "Soon. The spirits say the time is growing near."

"What *time*? Connor may not have any time left, Mitch. We have to find him *now*." Greg kicked at the blood stained snow.

"Trust me." Mitch stared intently at the doctor, his gaze demanding and firm.

Greg felt a twisting in his chest as deeply buried emotions stirred. He glared back, unwilling to let his natural instincts to stay in control be overruled.

Mitch continued to hold his gaze and quietly asked, "Have I not earned at least that much over these last three years?"

Feeling his carefully constructed walls of resistance crumble with the man's heart-felt plea, Greg surrendered. Giving an exasperated huff, he threw his hands in the air and sputtered, "Yes, of course, you have, but--."

"Soon then." Mitch firmly, but quietly cut off Greg's protest.

"All right! I trust you. With mine *and* Connor's lives." Frustrated, Greg gave the satisfied guide a suspicious glance. "You're not just trying to make me crazy with all this spirit talk and listening to the wind stuff, are you? Because you'd better know right now, I'm staying here, no matter what. You'll just have to put up with me, crazy or not."

Eyebrows raised and a smug smile tugging at his mouth, Mitch murmured, "I never said I was listening to the wind." He turned and walked away studying the packed ground for more clues.

Confused, Greg ran their conversation over in his mind and realized Mitch was right, he hadn't said that. Greg had imagined it all on his own. Seething at Mitch's receding back he called out, "See! I knew it! You *are* trying to make me nuts!"

Ignoring their conversation, the other men drew closer, examining the stains themselves. Several of them began searching the perimeter of the scene looking for tracks that led away from the site.

It only took a moment before Harry Bishop, a thickset, bear of a man who ran the post office and grocery store, called out, "Mitch! Come take a look at this. You're not going to believe your eyes. I sure as hell don't."

Covering the distance in a few graceful strides, Mitch squatted down beside Bishop and stared at the new tracks the man had uncovered. Preserved in the ice-hardened snow were several wolf paw prints.

But these weren't ordinary prints. They were huge, easily four times the size of a normal print. They were deep in a hard-packed drift, forced down through the frozen surface by a great weight.

Mitch stuck his hand down into the print and it swallowed his entire fist with room left over.

"What did you find?" When no one answered him, Greg squeezed in beside Bishop, crouched down by Mitch and looked for himself. He frowned and frantically searched the ground looking for evidence of smaller paw prints, normal sized prints, but found only a few more of the same kind. "What the hell made this? There aren't any wolves with paws this size."

"You're right. So it can't be real." Mitch pushed to his feet and brushed the crusted snow off his gloves. "Dark said he saw a skinwalker, a werewolf. Maybe what he saw was a man in wolf skins. I told you the Dena'ina are an ancient, isolated tribe. They still use the old ways. They wear animal headdresses, and use furs for winter robes. Two of them must have come across the accident," he pointed at a slightly smaller set of prints beside the huge ones, "and they took Dr. Jacy with them, like we thought. It's the only explanation that makes sense."

"And these prints?" Still hunched on the ground, Greg pressed one of his own fairly large hands into one of the prints and glared up at Mitch.

Mitch shrugged. "Just another part of the

ceremonial clothing, probably meant to scare away outsiders."

Bishop heaved up off the cold ground and stared at the trail of massive prints in the snow leading off to the north. "Well, it works. It scares me."

Straightening up, Greg pushed past the throng of curious men grouped around the prints and strode toward the snow machines. "Well, there's no reason to be scared."

He adjusted his goggles down and mounted his machine, then waited for Mitch and the rest of the men to do the same. "They had enough compassion to help Connor, they must not dislike outsiders that much." He started his engine and impatiently watched as Mitch slowly joined him and did the same. Greg called out as he gunned his engine. "Come on. Let's go. The light is fading."

Greg pulled out first, but let Mitch overtake him and lead the way, naturally falling into place at the guide's side. At this pace, if the weather held, they would reach the Dena'ani settlement just after nightfall.

***

Chapter Ten

Connor awoke to the now familiar sounds of Adam banking the fire, the scrape of metal rod on stone, and the crackle of dry wood being consumed by hungry flames. He was surprised at how content he felt. There was no lingering headache or nausea left over from his head injury this morning.

The hallucinations from last night were gone, too, just vivid memories dancing at the edge of his thoughts. The cabin room was distinct and clearly visible, and Adam was just Adam, tall, broad and mouth-wateringly gorgeous. But the memories of the visions made Connor uncomfortable. The harder he tried to examine them logically, the more they drifted away like the shadow dancers in his dreams had done.

Moving restlessly under the quilt to let Adam know he was awake, Connor looked over at his lover. He couldn't contain the pleased smile that stretched across his lips at the sight of the still naked man.

Standing up from his crouch by the fire, Adam rose to his full height and flexed his upper body. His thick cock hung proudly between his legs, balanced on its hefty, dark, round sac. It tapped against his heavily muscled thighs as he walked to the bed to gather Connor into his arms for a spine tingling, arousing, good morning kiss that stole all Connor's strength.

Needing to draw in an extra deep breath to refill his depleted lungs, Connor opened his eyes and stared up at Adam. Soft black eyes looked down at him, the

corners crinkling, Adam's gaze gentle and full of love.
Connor's heart leapt, missing a beat, at the depth of
devotion he saw. It both unnerved and thrilled him.
This man truly loved him, affecting him in a way no one
else ever had.

He licked his lips, savoring the slightly salty
taste of the man. "Morning."

"You are awake. I grew concerned." Adam
stroked Connor's disheveled hair from his face, letting
his hand linger, fingers lacing into the pale strands and
staying there.

Shrugging, Connor leaned into the caress.
"Why? You just wore me out last night." He ran both
hands across Adam's hard chest, lightly rubbing over
his taut nipples again and again. "I think modern
science is underestimating the medicinal value of good
sex." His hands dipped lower and caressed the rippled
muscles of the man's washboard abdomen. Adam's
gaze took on a lustful gleam and his breathing became
shallow and rapid, matching Connor's. "I feel great this
morning." Connor felt blood rise to his face, heat
radiating from it. A little shyly he added, "And so do
you. Feel great, I mean."

"I'm pleased." Adam dropped a quick kiss on
the tip of Connor's nose. "The spirits have been helping
you heal. It is no longer morning. Soon the moon will
rise and the bonding ceremony will begin."

"I slept the entire day? Wow, you really did
wear me out." Connor let the blankets drift down to his
waist, amazed at how warm the room still was.

Connor's thoughts filled with the memories of
last night and the bizarre visions flowed into his mind.

"Last night… last night I saw some things, hallucinations, I –I think. Probably a side effect of my concussion. But they're still things I need explained. Just in case," he swallowed hard and looked up at Adam for reassurance, "in case they happen again."

"All will be explained as the time becomes right, adada." Adam nibbled at the curve of Connor's shoulder, and kissed a trail of delicate pecks up his neck making Connor shiver, his skin tingling wherever Adam's hot, moist lips touched.

When the kisses turned into the licking and sucking of his ear and jaw, Connor choked out a weak protest, "That's not much of an answer."

He arched, crushing his chest to Adam's, his arms wrapped around the man's wide shoulders while his fingers dug into his lover's strapping biceps.

A soft, seductive whisper blew in Connor's ear. "It is all I have to give. Remember my words from last night and trust in me, Connor. I am yours for all time."

"I-I know." Eyes closed, overwhelmed by the sensations Adam was causing in his body and his heart, Connor shook his head. "But this ceremony? It means we're committing to each other, right? Like a marriage?" He shivered and rapidly shook his head, making tiny, confused, negative gestures. "I'm not sure about this."

Hands in Connor's hair, Adam stilled his movement, his voice gentle, but firm. "You allowed our spirits to join last night. The commitment has already been made."

Slowly sliding his fingers out of Connor's hair, Adam sat up on the edge of the bed and began

135

unbraiding the lock of his own rich, black hair that held the two silver bands.

"Tonight's ceremony is ritual, to honor the spirit world that has brought us together and forged our destinies into one." Pulling one silver band tied on a thin leather lacing from his hair, Adam knotted the ends together to make a necklace.

"There is no going back for either of us. Your spirits surged with joy to bond with mine. I know your true heart. Now you must accept it as well."

Leaning down he slipped the lacing over Connor's head and hung it around his neck, positioning the band over Connor's heart.

Swallowing past the growing lump in his throat, eyes glued to the ring on his pale skin, Connor whispered, "That's asking a lot."

"Nothing more than I have already given you." Adam sealed his mouth over the ring and kissed Connor's chest. He worked his way up Connor's body until he could kiss him, his lips insistent, but gentle and thorough, making the embrace deep and hot.

Connor's mind reeled. His thoughts were scrambled, trying to find some logical order to the events happening so quickly in his suddenly changing life.

Despite his fears, Connor didn't object to what Adam wanted. He did love this man. Adam was exactly the kind of man Connor had been looking for -- strong, sensitive and nurturing. The way he had cared for Connor since his accident had shown him that first-hand. Adam was a man with deeply rooted loyalties and a quiet self-assurance that was unflappable. Add the facts that he was a bronzed, god-like man to look at and a superman in bed, and Adam Lowell was Connor Jacy's dream man come to life.

So why was he so nervous? Was it the daunting thought of how to work out a committed relationship when he was a doctor, needed in a town hundreds of miles away and Adam was a reclusive trapper, part of a tribe in a secluded territory? Or was it the reoccurring mystic visions and the ancient shadow dancers invading their bedroom each night?

Still entangled in Adam's unyielding arms, with their tongues down each other's throats, Connor decided to listen to his heart instead of his mind for once. Surging up, he threw himself into the embrace with an energy and ravenous desire that belied his earlier reservations.

Adam groaned and pressed Connor closer, plastering their bodies together in a heated embrace so intense Connor thought they would melt and merge into one.

Whatever the reason he was nervous, Connor pushed it to the back of his mind. They could work out the details of their life later. Tonight was a time to celebrate and be introduced to Adam's world. They would seal their commitment in the eyes of the tribe. Connor would worry about his own people when the time came.

Breaking the kiss, Adam drew back slightly. He reverently touched the silver ring on his lover's heaving chest.

"I will braid this into your hair during the ritual of the moon. It will be for all to see, a symbol of our joining, our eternal bond."

Connor blinked back an unexpected rush of moisture behind his eyes. It made the firelight shimmer, distorting his sight. Suddenly Adam swayed and blurred, his face and body replaced with the image from last night, the vision of the wolf superimposed on the man.

Connor gasped and pulled back as far as Adam's substantial body weight would allow him. The wolf vision wasn't vicious or threatening, but Connor knew he wasn't under the influence of outside forces, like the iqemik or shock, anymore. He shouldn't be seeing things.

As quickly as it came, the vision faded, leaving nothing but questions behind. Connor blinked and Adam became Adam again, waiting with a strangely calm, expectant look on his face.

Connor blushed and stammered. "Last night... and-and right now, I keep seeing you with a wolf." He shook his head and tried again. "No that's not right. I-I... keep seeing you *as* a wolf, a huge wolf. One that stands on its back legs. Like a... like a werewolf."

He snorted at his own ridiculous words and squirmed under Adam's heavy weight, both comforted and unnerved by it. Rational thought tried to form an explanation. "Is that your spirit totem I'm imagining or something?"

Expression neutral, Adam leaned down and kissed Connor's eyes closed. "Why must you be imagining it?"

"Why?" Connor snorted and huffed out a hollow laugh. "Because I have a concussion. You've been burning iqemik." Panting, Connor arched his spine and let Adam have access to more of his neck, his body reacting to the slow teasing kisses and long, wet licks over his flesh. His voice became strained and needy.

"And if you must know, I think you have a feral, animalistic nature I find very arousing." His fingers kneaded the flesh under his hands. He began to return the kisses in kind, devouring every inch of skin he could reach between breathless sentences. "I'm projecting my fantasy onto you. I imagined you were a wolf last night, too."

Adam leisurely kissed Connor, a slow, gentle exploration of mouth and lips, full of love and tender romance. When Connor became weak and pliant in his arms, he broke off and sat up, chastely pulling the blanket up over Connor's waist.

"My people call a man in a wolf's skin, a skinwalker. There are many ways to become a skinwalker, a werewolf."

Breathless and dazed, Connor muttered, "I thought legend says you have to be bitten by one."

"That is one way to be blessed, yes." Adam reached up and rubbed his left shoulder and neck as a flash of a long past memory resurfaced.

"Blessed?" Connor's eyebrows arched high.

Adam nodded solemnly. "To my people it is an honor to be granted immortality. To be given the power to keep the natural world in balance for all creatures that walk upon it."

Connor frowned, his voice dubious. "It seems like a pretty harsh way to get 'honored'."

Adam smiled indulgently and caressed the line of Connor's jaw. "There are other, less painful ways, to be blessed by the ancient ones. The spiritwalkers can enter a man's dreams, bringing him a vision of the wolf spirit on a vision quest. A man could become a skinwalker by drinking from a wolf's print or if he is called upon by the wolf spirit through ancient ritual."

Remembering the shadow dancers from last night, Connor shivered and pulled the blanket higher. "Seems like a lot of spirit work involved." He glanced around at the darkening corners of the room. "I think you guys spend too much time burning iqemik."

Chuckling, Adam rose and walked back to the fire, adding another log to the blaze. He gave Connor an unfathomable glance over his shoulder. "Of course, there is always the more pleasant way to be blessed and honored by the spirit world with the gift of a skinwalker's spirit."

Adam gracefully rose to his feet, all power and sinewy strength in his smooth movements. Never breaking eye contact, he shrugged into his clothing and thick, deer-hide coat.

The mysterious tone of Adam's voice tweaked Connor's attention even more than his words did. "Pleasant? What way's that?"

Adam turned from the fire, and leveled an intense, penetrating stare at Connor. "By having sex with a werewolf."

From the angle Connor was sitting, the light must have caught Adam's eyes just right because they now glowed the same rusty orange as before and stayed that color.

Out There in the Night

Speechless, Connor was mesmerized by the man's powerful, sensuous movements, as the memory of last night's wild lovemaking and distorted visions replayed in his mind.

"That is, having sex with a werewolf and surviving." Pausing at the door, Adam's tone became rough with unspoken meaning as he added, "How alive do you feel this evening, adada?"

With that, he walked out the door just as Connor realized Adam's back had been to the fire the whole time his eyes had appeared to glow. The orange color couldn't have been a reflection of the flames.

***

Just after nightfall, Adam returned to the cabin, a small bundle tucked under one arm and several black body paint markings on his face. He entered the room to find Connor standing in the middle of the cabin, the old quilt from the bed wrapped tightly around his body.

Connor snapped around at the sound of the door, a dismayed, startled look on his lightly bruised face.

"There you are." Connor's shoulders relaxed and he let out a long breath through pursed lips. "I-I think I have a little problem. I found the bucket to relieve myself in and I found the food you left for me, but I can't find my clothes. I don't think this," he flashed open the quilt and then closed it more tightly around his naked body, pulling the quilt in against the sudden chill, "is exactly the way I should greet the tribe for the first time."

Adam gave his mate an appreciative leer. "You may be surprised, Connor. We're very comfortable with our natural forms." He set his bundle down on the table and took Connor in his arms and murmured. "I think you would make a very memorable impression like that."

Connor laughed and leaned into Adam's embracing strength, a thrill of re-ignited desire flowing through his veins at the big native's mere touch. Adam's clean, woodsy, masculine scent filled Connor's senses and his cock stirred in response.

Blackening a thumb by running it through the marking on his forehead, Adam wordlessly showed Connor the smudge of paint before he firmly painted a few brisk strokes over Connor's forehead and cheeks, marking him in a mirror image of his own face.

"Now, you're almost perfect." Adam blew a sultry purr into Connor's ear, then tongued the outer shell.

The unfamiliar smell of the body paint made Connor's nose twitch. He wrinkled his nose, then gave his unpredictable lover a mock pout. "Almost perfect?"

Quick as a rattler striking, Adam snaked a large, callused hand under the opening of the quilt and palmed Connor's semi-flaccid cock. It responded to the direct attention immediately, instantly hardening and lengthening. Adam smiled, then whispered, "Now, you're perfect."

A small gasp escaped Connor's parted lips. He pressed closer to Adam, giving into his body's desires without hesitation. He imagined the sounds of drums again in the background, and his hips began a ragged dance of encouragement in time to the ancient beat.

Adam firmly fondled and palmed the growing flesh. He grinned at Connor, rewarding him with a slow, sensuous pump-and-squeeze motion that made Connor weak in the knees.

A few more strokes and Connor knew he would lose control, but before he could warn Adam, the big man dropped to his knees and swallowed Connor's cock to the root, sucking the rigid shaft down in one smooth, lightening-quick, hard motion.

Dropping the quilt and grabbing onto Adam's shoulders, Connor cried out and exploded. His climax was so unexpected and powerful he could feel it boiling up from his balls and coursing through every inch of his shaft. Each spurt and pulse of his cum was like breathing fire out of his cock. The tip burned and spasmed as if he was giving birth as he emptied himself into Adam's greedy throat. It was a terrifying mix of startling pain and delicious ecstasy.

The sure knowledge he had just given Adam more than his cum flashed across Connor's jumbled mind. He had ejaculated a part of his soul, as well. A part he could never reclaim.

Releasing the shrinking cock from his lips, Adam stood and pulled Connor into a deep kiss. His hands kneaded the rounded globes of the man's ass, tightly pressing Connor's spent groin and stomach against his own straining and needy cock.

Regaining some of his strength, Connor reluctantly tore away from the passionate, demanding kiss. His hands flew to Adam's pants and scrabbled at the laces. The iron shaft directly under them bulged against the ties, making it hard to loosen them. After several fumbled attempt, fingers more practiced at removing the laces joined Connor's hands.

Soon the pants were on the floor and under Connor's knees as he followed them down. Connor stared at Adam's proud cock, memorizing its details, wanting to know every detail by sight, as well as by taste and feel.

The shaft was huge, thicker at the base and heavily veined. It bobbed and strained, curving up and out from Adam's taut, defined, muscular body. The uncircumcised foreskin was like a large hood, jacketing the mushroom-shaped head in deep folds of cinnamon flesh. It was darker than the rest of the shaft, and as Connor pulled it back, he found it extended all the way down to the base. He pulled it back several times like a sleeve, and then released it to trail his hands over the rest of Adam's solid groin. Adam's heavy breathing and a slight thrusting of his hips re-ignited Connor's own libido and he felt his cock stir again.

Tracing the hollows of Adam's thighs, Connor's hands dipped lower and traveled to the dark thatch of black hair surrounding the shaft and its sac. Connor tugged at the dangling pouch, excited by the way it drew up and grew heavier in his hand.

Leaning forward, he tentatively licked at the wrinkled pouch. Tasting and exploring the surface, he slowly worked his tongue up to the base of Adam's cock. Slightly dizzy from the excitement and the heat of the room, Connor rested his head against Adam's belly for support for a moment. A heavy, soothing hand came down to rest on his head and his dizziness magically receded, ebbing away in time to the drum beat in his head.

Pulling back the ponderous foreskin, Connor began placing quick, little, wet licks all around the underside of the tip of Adam's cock. A guttural hum of pleasure vibrated down from above, transmitted through Adam's abdomen to Connor's resting head.

Somewhere nearby, Connor heard soft flutes playing. The song was light and eerie, and the melody hypnotic. It sounded close to Connor, but muted, like he was hearing it through a layer of cotton batting.

Strong, restless hands fell on Connor's shoulders. Adam's fingers rubbed at the base of his neck, kneading the muscles and silently encouraging him to do more.

Not wanting to rush this first time, but anxious to taste Adam, Connor lapped at the top of the head with the flat of his tongue, his mouth forming a loose, wet ring around the bulb's edge. Every bob and twist teased lightly over the sensitive skin, brushing wetly along its underside with the delicate, moist tissues of Connor's inner lips.

Connor closed his eyes against a new wave of dizziness, concentrating on tugging and fondling the tightly drawn-up sac between Adam's parted thighs. His free hand clung to the massive man's sturdy hip for support.

A deep, growling moan from above sent a thrill of lust directly to Connor's cock and a chill down his spine. He longed to touch his own straining cock, but refused to move either hand from his lover, using one to give pleasure and one for much needed support.

Working his mouth over the straining cock, Connor savored the few drops of cum leaking out of the slit. He swallowed only after he had pressed the flat of his tongue hard against the shaft and rubbed the slick fluid onto his taste buds, enjoying the feel of the hot, iron-hard cock and the bitter tang of his lover together.

Nose pressed close, Connor inhaled the scent of musk and sweat from Adam's groin, and a shiver of ravenous desire skittered down his spine. Driven by a sudden burning need to bring Adam to climax as soon as possible, Connor sucked the head and as much of the thick shaft as he could take into his mouth. Swallowing and sucking, he laved his tongue around it, flicking the tip against the underside and tracing the path of the large, pounding veins ridging the shaft.

Adam's hands moved to fist in Connor's tousled, blond hair, but they neither pulled nor shoved at him, merely held onto him. Connor was aware that the mighty palms were careful to never come close to the healing wounds on either side of his head.

Hips thrusting in a controlled rhythm, Adam growled through bared teeth and threw his head back. Connor looked up as he sucked and followed the line of Adam's neck and jaw to see an expression of animal lust contort the man's handsome, angular face. Connor sucked harder and Adam bucked once and went rigid, climaxing into Connor's eager throat, letting out a roar that sounded part snarl and part howl.

Swallowing the rich, bitter cum, Connor slowly released the still hard rod. It swayed and thickened, arching regally out from Adam's chiseled body. Connor kissed the tip and rose shakily to his feet, guided by Adam's strong hands.

Once he regained his feet, Adam pulled Connor into a hungry, demanding kiss. It made his skin flush and his already cloudy mind spin. The room swam and the strange odor from the smudge markings tickled Connor's nose again. Connor's knees weakened and he was momentarily dependent on Adam to hold him up.

Breaking the kiss, but keeping an arm securely around Connor's waist, Adam tilted his young lover's face back and looked deep into his glazed green eyes.

"The bonding ritual has begun. We have tasted of each other's life force, planted the seeds of forever. We are as one."

The drums in the distance grew louder and Connor blinked to clear his head, realizing the drums were coming from outside the cabin instead of in his head. His vision blurred again and the firelight cast elongated shadows that seemed to dance and sway to the beat on the wall behind Adam.

To Connor, Adam was a solid vision of god-like proportions, tall, broad and every inch the native warrior. He was naked, his skin lightly oiled, shining in the firelight, and the tribal markings on his handsome face made him appear fierce, raw and decidedly primal in Connor's eyes. The caring and deep affection in Adam's loving expression made Connor's heart pound and his breathing quicken.

Unable to stop, Connor blurted out, "I love you." He bit his tongue, then shook his head, his eyes never leaving Adam's, surprised by his own outburst. "I didn't think I could, not after just knowing you for a few days, but I do. I *really* do. I love you." Connor whispered and shook his head again. "To hell with all the complications. I want you. Just you, always you."

Adam tightened his hold on his mate. "It is as the spiritwalkers have foretold. Our time is now and forever."

Connor pulled Adam's head down and kissed him, a soft, thorough, fervent kiss, full of promise and expectations of a future together.

Adam returned the kiss with equal ardor, lifting Connor off the floor with the strength of his enthusiasm. The kiss went on and on until a series of mournful, erratic drumbeats from outside broke the passionate spell, a not so subtle reminder they were expected elsewhere.

Drawing back, Adam cupped Connor's face in his hands after setting him back down on the floor. "Soon you will witness the blessing of the spiritwalkers for yourself, adada. But you will need something more than your skin to greet them in."

Adam ignored his own naked state, and opened the bundle he had brought. It contained new clothes for Connor. A jerkin and lace-up pants similar to Adam's own. Both were made from soft, supple elk hide. The bundle also held a full-length, black fur robe. Adam wrapped the robe around his own broad shoulders, carelessly dismissing his naked state beneath it.

Adam handed the clothing to Connor, pride and pleasure in his eyes. "A gift of welcome for you from my people."

Connor took the offered presents. "These are amazing, Adam. How did they have the time to do this? I'm honored."

Out There in the Night

There were symbols and patterns burnt into the pieces of clothing, the same markings as on Adam's silver bands. The workmanship was intricate, painstakingly worked along the edges of the jerkin and down the sides of the pants. Connor recognized one as a match to the black, smelly marking on their foreheads. Many were the symbol he knew stood for the moon in the native culture.

Gait growing unsteady with the return of a new wave of dizziness, Connor needed Adam to help him get dressed.

Adam helped him smooth down the jerkin over the pants and then pulled a pair of thick, soft, high-topped moccasins from the bottom of the bundle. He helped Connor pull them on and lace them up when Connor's fingers fumbled clumsily with the ties.

Between the energy-draining event of having a spine-melting orgasm and the effort of getting dressed for the first time in days, Connor was exhausted and light-headed by the time they were finished. He found himself leaning more and more on Adam for support, but he had no intention of missing this ceremony. Connor wanted Adam with all his heart.

"I think I can do this on my own, thanks."

Standing straighter, Connor pulled away from Adam and walked to the cabin door with exaggerated care. The room shimmered and swayed with each unsure step he took. He drew in a deep breath to steady himself, but his head filled with the sharp scent of the body paint and the room spun faster. Adam instantly appeared at his side and wrapped an arm around his waist, and the room stopped swaying and merely shimmered in the firelight.

Glancing up at Adam's concerned but serene face, Connor gave a wry smile. "Okay, maybe not *all* on my own."

Once outside, Connor's head cleared a little, but he held fast to Adam for both emotional and physical support. The sharp bite of the cold winds blew away some of the haziness in his mind, but his vision was still impaired.

Adam led him across a wide stretch of open, snow-covered ground toward a large bonfire blazing in the middle of a ring of large stones. They passed through a gathering of more than two dozen Native American men and women, all dressed in long, fur robes and heavy, intricate headdresses made from the skins of wolves, their bodies mostly hidden from view. Their faces were painted in various colors, the patterns all different, but still strangely familiar to Connor. Many of them played small drums or long wooden flutes, and some rattled dried gourds creating an eerie backdrop for the starlight night. Connor found the eerie mix unnerving and primal, but entrancingly beautiful.

The tribe wordlessly parted to let Adam and Connor pass, then sealed the circle back up around them. In front of the large fire stood an older native had never seen before. Still tall and broad, his face showed the passage of time in its weathered creases and deeply bronzed skin. His penetrating, dark eyes told of many mysteries seen over the years. Wisdom and great knowledge were reflected in the kind, but intense gaze he leveled at Connor.

Assuming this was the tribe's medicine man and

the official overseer of the ritual, Connor bowed his head slightly out of respect. Dyami grunted a pleased sound, and Adam tugged Connor down to kneel on a large bear fur lying at the medicine man's feet. Adam knelt beside him, his arm still around Connor's waist.

The flutes joined the rattle of the gourds and the pounding rhythm of the drums rose up from the warriors surrounding them. Taking a small pot from under his robe, Dyami chanted in guttural, singsong rhythm while he layered more symbols on both Connor's and Adam's upturned faces, this time in red.

The smell from the paint was even stronger than before. Confused, Connor watched the warriors began to twirl and dance, their feet never seeming to touch the ground. Sudden enlightenment hit and Connor realized the paint was mixed with a strong hallucinogen he was absorbing through his skin.

Panicked, he turned to Adam, but saw the same faraway, glazed look in his lover's dark eyes that he knew must be mirrored in his own. As he stared at Adam, the man's face wavered and changed, elongating and growing darker.

The chanting and music flared, ringing out clear and crisp in the starless night, the rhythm pulsing. All around him, the warriors' dance intensified, the drum beat thumping in Connor's head and chest. The warriors' robes seemed to melt into their flesh and their wolf headdresses merged with their own human faces. In the time it took for Connor to take in a ragged breath of astonishment, he and Adam were surrounded by a pack of huge, painted beasts.

Connor's wide-eyed stare darted back to his

lover, knowing what he would see. A wolf's muzzle and glowing orange eyes replaced Adam's sharp-boned features. Adam's sleek, black hair covered his entire body as fur and sharp-fanged teeth marked his lip. A deep snarling growl rumbled deep in his throat.

Connor blinked hard, his breathing rapid and labored, startled by the visions, but not truly frightened by them any more.

The black wolf's teeth flashed, and then the wolf shifted, but this time it wasn't back to Adam's normal appearance. Its body grew broader and taller, more like a man covered from head-to-toe in a skin-tight wolf's hide. The beast remained kneeling beside Conner, but its size now dwarfed him.

Oddly unfazed by the startling transformation, Conner continued to stare. Mesmerized by the rusty orange eyes, he rested one hand on the beast's chest and the familiar beat of his lover's heart thundered in his ears. He touched the animal's muzzle and sensed Adam's spirit dwelling within the massive skull.

"Adam? It is you, isn't it? Is this a dream or the drugs?" Connor hesitantly fingered the silver band still braided into the thick, black hair by the beast's face and then touched the matching band hanging around his own neck. Awe-struck, Connor suddenly knew the truth. "This is real, isn't it?"

In answer, the beast reached out and pulled Connor closer, a gentle power in its cautious grip.

Connor stared at the orange eyes for a moment longer then tentatively laid his head against the beast's chest and listened. As the familiar sound of Adam's heartbeat vibrated in his ear, Connor relaxed into the embrace and returned it. "You're real."

The world spun and blurred around him, chaotic and jumbled, with harsh sounds and eerie tribal beats, but Connor felt it all wash away, tucked securely in Adam's arms. He was surrounded by overwhelming joy and contentment, engulfed by it, his heart and spirit consumed in the blazing hot flames of Adam's limitless desire and deep love for him.

Connor had never been so happy, or so scared. He was in love with a werewolf, an ancient, spirit-guided werewolf. He couldn't grasp the enormity of what the situation would mean to his life, all he knew right now was that he was where he was meant to be, with the man he was meant to spend the rest of his life with.

***

Chapter Eleven

Mitch had warned them they would be approaching the Dena'ani settlement shortly after nightfall, but the trip had been delayed when Mitch developed a problem with his snow machine. It took the guide almost an hour of patient tinkering with the engine before he got it running again and the search team could continue on its way.

Greg had grown restless and anxious after the first thirty minutes of repairs. He grumbled and stomped, but the guide would not be rushed. Mitch merely gave his usual mysterious, tolerant smile and continued working. Greg rewarded him with an evil glare and a prolonged view of his backside. Mitch didn't seem to mind.

The other team members had used the time to eat and refuel the machines. When that was completed, they checked their weapons, as the distant howl of several wolves carried on the brisk winds, lending unease to the falling twilight.

Now they were back on the trail and making good time on the hard-packed snow, despite the fierce winds that had picked up once they neared the small settlement.

Just ahead, Greg could see the glow of a large bonfire. As he got closer, he could make out the forms of a large number of people around the fire. It looked like they were in the midst of a native ceremony of some kind. Over the roar of the winds and the engines of the snow machines, Greg could hear the beat of drums and the distinctive sound of the howling of a pack of wolves, eerie and mournful in the darkness. The sound sent a chill up his spine and a sharp tingle to his groin.

Mitch stopped his machine and Greg pulled up next to him. The other men slowed and pulled up on either side of them. They all stared at the dancing natives by the bonfire.

Greg caught a slight movement out of the corner of his eye and he turned to watch as Mitch closed his eyes and cocked his head to one side to let the winds blow through his loosened hair.

"What? What do you hear?" Greg leaned closer and tried to listen to whatever had Mitch's attention. All he could hear was the howling winds picking up force and a few snatches of drumbeats.

"This is a sacred ceremony." Mitch pointed at the distant circle of dancing figures. "We should wait. It is almost complete."

"What kind of ceremony?" Greg squinted and tried to see through the crowd of swirling forms. A flash of yellow-white caught his attention and he strained forward to try to see better, but a strong hand on his shoulder restrained him. Greg darted a sour glare at Mitch, but the guide didn't remove his hand.

"They're all fur and feathers." Greg shook his head and hunched into the wind, the sharp sting of its power bringing tears to his eyes and distorting his vision. "They look like wolves. Those headdresses make them look so real." Greg grabbed his binoculars out of a coat pocket and focused on the dancers.

"Really real." He voice dropped an octave lower, tainted with disbelief. "I don't know what they are, but I...I don't think they're in costumes."

"Of course, they are. It is ancient ceremonial dress. Let me see." Mitch grabbed for the binoculars, but Greg ducked away and evaded his grasp.

One large, broad form in the center of the circle of dancers attracted Greg's attention. The figure looked up and seemed to glance in the search party's direction while Greg focused on him. The creature bared its teeth and a vicious snarl distorted its face, its muzzle wrinkling as it scented the air.

Startled, Greg blinked and rubbed his eyes with a gloved hand and looked again. Just as his sight cleared, a gap opened in the crowd and the flash of yellow-white was revealed to be a head of blond hair. Dropping the binoculars down to hang around his neck, Greg gunned his snow machine.

Mitch's hand tightened on Greg's shoulder. The guide had to shout to be heard over the sudden roar of the sled's engine. "Wait! Stay here!"

"Like hell!" Greg released the brake and inched forward out of Mitch's reach. "That thing has Connor!"

Overtop of sounds of wailing winds and ticking engines, a sudden chorus of howling could be heard. The urgent caterwauling spurred Greg into action. He gunned his machine and shot past Mitch, ignoring the muffled shouts of warning. Several of the other men followed his lead and moved towards the circle of dancing figures.

As the snow machines approached the circle, Greg headed straight toward the snarling form near

156

Connor. He watched the beast rise up taller and hover menacingly over the young doctor.

Greg's glance fell to Connor who seemed dazed, strangely unaffected by the chaos and commotion all around him.

Crouching low, the snarling figure grabbed at Connor. Greg accelerated and impulsively aimed the sled at the creature in an effort to drive it away from his friend.

Fighting a sudden gust of blinding winds, Greg forced his snow machine through the throng of figures circling the fire, never noticing the howling, snapping forms had shifted from walking on two legs to running on four. He had a clear shot at the creature menacing Connor. He drove straight at the massive, black beast with the bright orange eyes.

The shouts and noise from the approaching rescue team seemed to stir Connor from his dazed state. Just before Greg slammed into his target, Connor rallied and hurled himself to one side, shoving Adam out of the path of the advancing sled.

Weak and unsteady, with unfamiliar drugs in his system, Connor's rescue attempt wasn't completely successful. The snow machine hit both Adam and Connor. The impact pulled the werewolf Adam down beneath the weight of the sled and forced Connor to one side.

Landing on the edge of the fire ring, Connor struck his head on the rocks encircling the crackling blaze and lay still. Disturbed by the force of his fall, glowing-hot embers spit out of the fire and landed on Connor's chest, several spilling down the front of his jerkin to smolder against unprotected flesh.

Veering to the left, Greg stopped his sled and rushed to Connor's side, dragging him away from the fire. Greg feverishly worked to brush the sizzling coals from Connor's skin, shoving a handful of packed snow down on top of the resulting burns.

Looking wildly around for any sign of the huge beast, Greg's heart thundered in his chest. Everywhere he looked chaos and madness surrounded him. A pack of large wolves had joined the dancers at some point, and now there was nothing but wolves all around him. The cloaked natives had all disappeared in the chaotic jumble of the ceremony and the influx of the search team. The large beast he had seen attacking Connor was nowhere to be seen. Only a very large black wolf lay unmoving in the snow, several yards away from the snow machine.

Scrambling to his feet, Greg grabbed an unconscious Connor under his arms and began dragging him to his sled. The burden suddenly became easier as a new pair of hands lifted Connor's limp legs in the air. Greg looked up to see Mitch's pinched, unhappy expression.

Relieved at the sight of his guide, but still angry with Mitch for trying to slow him down earlier, Greg barked out, "What the fuck happened here, Mitch? What the hell kind of ceremony was this?"

"I told you to wait!" Mitch grunted and lifted Connor onto the sled, then helped Greg hurriedly strap Connor to the stretcher sled towed behind his own machine. "Don't you ever listen to anyone else besides yourself?"

"That '*thing*' was going to attack Connor!" Greg spat out, bristling. He worked frantically to do a quick assessment of Connor's physical state and get the injured man out of the turbulent area as soon as humanly possible. "He was in trouble!"

Looking at the injured doctor's pale skin and lackluster, dazed eyes when Greg pulled up Connor's eyelids to check his pupils, Mitch thundered back, "Well, not as much as he's in right now!"

"I didn't have a choice!" Oddly, Greg was hurt Mitch might think less of him for this. "How was I supposed to know he'd try to get in the way? He looked dazed! If he could move, why didn't he try to get away?"

"Did you ever think that maybe he didn't want to?" Leaving Greg speechless for once, Mitch ran to the other side of the sled and secured the last of the ties holding Connor in place.

The other search members were chasing off the wolves, keeping them from coming too near Greg and Mitch. An occasional wolf would venture near, but it was driven back each time.

The large, black wolf still hadn't moved. Greg glanced nervously at it while working on Connor. Mitch followed Greg's gaze with his eyes. Pushing up from the sled, he pulled his rifle from its sleeve on his machine and gestured at his seat.

"Go! Get a head start. Take the boy back to the clinic. I'll take your sled and join up with you in a few miles."

Greg straddled the seat and automatically started the engine, even while protesting the move.

"Nobody needs to stay behind." He hurried glanced around at the surrounding mayhem, noting that most of the wolves were gone. The few that remained were hovering protectively near the downed black wolf.

"Let's just leave." Greg's handsome face pinched into a worried frown. "All of us!"

"Dr. Jacy's life is in your hands now! Don't argue! Get going!" Mitch slapped him on the back and quickly turned away, refusing to let Greg argue.

Several of the other team members had rejoined them. They formed a semi-circle around the stretcher sled, blocking the few remaining wolves from approaching. Rifles were raised but they all pointed in the air.

If the animals remained at a distance, the men wouldn't fire. They all knew the balance of nature was a finely-honed scale and the wolves were a necessary part of the ecosystem here.

Mitch ran to the stopped snow machine driven by Deputy Joss Crow. He grabbed the man by the arm and yelled to be heard over the noise of the engines, the screaming winds and the howling of the wolves in the distance.

"Head out, Joss. I'll bring up the rear and make sure none of them follow." He cocked his head at the snarling wolves pacing near their downed pack mate. "Take my docs home. I'll make sure you get out of here without any interference."

"You sure, Mitch?" Joss eyed the small pack then darted a worried glance at Connor's sled. "I don't want to leave you, but Dr. Jacy didn't look so good."

"I'm just going to hold them off until you get out

of here. I'll catch up in a few minutes. Get going before the big one wakes up. He'll be trouble, he looks like their alpha."

Joss nodded and hit the gas, gesturing for the rest of the team to follow him. He took up a position beside Greg, and the doctor gave in to his command to pull out.

After casting a worried look over his shoulder at Mitch, Greg reluctantly headed out. The rest of the team flanked the sled when possible, all moving as fast as the terrain would allow them.

***

Mitch waited until they were out of sight, then turned back to face the pack. He was confronted with three Dena'ina warriors, the oldest bearing the markings of a medicine man. The old one knelt at the fallen black wolf's side.

Not the least bit surprised at the sudden change in the wolves' appearances, Mitch knelt down beside the old man and placed a hand on the wolf's flank. "Is he gravely harmed?"

Dyami shook his head and sighed. "No. The injury is small. He will awaken soon."

"When he does, tell him I will help the spirits watch over his mate. The boy was re-injured in the attempt to protect his mate from the snow machine. He needs their medical attention now." Mitch pushed up off the ground, but remained standing protectively near the downed leader.

The old one placed a charm on the black wolf's

head and looked up at Mitch. "The moon will be full in only a few days and their spirits have already merged. The bonding is complete." He waved a hand in the direction the search team had taken. "The boy has only until the crest of full moon to learn to accept his place beside his mate before his change occurs."

"Hopefully that will be time enough to make him whole again." Mitch couldn't keep a small hint of pride out of his voice. "The tall, dark one is a very skilled healer." His expression twisted into an exasperated grimace as he thought about recent events. "Even if he doesn't listen very well."

The black wolf stirred, his legs twitching against the ground, but he didn't raise his head or open his eyes.

Mitch walked to his snow machine. He shot two rounds into the air, then mounted the sled and started it, calling out to the old man, "When the time is right to reclaim his mate, I will make sure Dr. Jacy is be ready for him."

He headed out in the direction the rest of the search team had taken. Mitch pushed his machine to its limit, making good enough time to rejoin the others within a few miles. The small risk of rapid speed on the uneven terrain had been worth it when he saw the grudging look of relief on Greg's face as he pulled up beside him.

With a short jerky nod at Joss, Mitch took over his place as lead scout, and Greg fell into place at his side once again.

***

Chapter Twelve

Slowly waking, the smell of disinfectant and bleached sheets helped Connor identify where he was more than anything else did. Through watery slits, his first sight was a soft blue, thermal blanket, like the ones they used at the clinic. He experimented by moving a leg and some of the bumps under the blanket shifted slightly. He appeared to be in one piece, despite what the blinding pain in his head and the sharp burning in his chest told him.

The room began to waver. Connor sighed and closed his eyes for a moment, trying to stop the spinning before the all-too-familiar nausea rose up from his churning stomach.

His head ached, both inside and out. The right side of his skull burned. A now-familiar burn told him he had yet another laceration to add to his list of wounds for the week. The inside of his head felt as if a buzz saw had been used to slice through his brain, leaving mangled, bloody bits slogging around in his skull, every severed nerve screaming in pain.

He cautiously coaxed his eyes open again, and looked around, careful not to move his head. Although there were four beds in the ward room, it was only illuminated by two over bed back lights, one behind his bed and one behind the bed opposite his.

The other bed was an organized tangle of tubing, wires and drainage tubes, the patient a mass of bandages and casts. Connor lifted his head slightly to see over the footboard better. As his head rose up off the pillow, a familiar, if weak voice forced the events of the last few days to instantly snap into focus.

"Welcome back, young one. They were worried for a time you might not return from your spirit walk."

"Dark! You're alive!" Connor tried to surge up off the bed, but the pounding behind his eyes and a sudden surge of nausea overruled him. He winced and folded back against the mattress, pale and shaky from the effort. "I thought you were, I mean... Adam said you were dead."

"Adam?" Dark's face clouded, momentarily, then relaxed. "The big Dena'ina warrior from the accident?"

Stunned, Connor's forehead furrowed despite the pain it caused and his eyes filled with hurt. "Yes, Adam. I can't believe he'd lie to me about something like that."

Raising a hand in a halting motion, palm out and fingers pointing at the ceiling, Dark calmed Connor's fears. "Do not mistrust him. Your mate thought I was dying. The spirits did call to me, but I refused to go."

"I always knew you were a tough guy." Conner smiled through his grimace of pain and let the sudden burst of despair that tried to enter his heart drift away. He ignored the other man's reference to his 'mate'. "What happened to you after the accident? I can't remember anything about it."

"I made my way back." Dark simplified the explanation in his usual brief way. He was a man who conserved his words on a regular basis. "Dr. Pierce and the new lady doctor, Dr. Webb, saved my life."

"Webb was the *woman*?" Connors eyebrows hit his hairline, but the painful tugging on his suture line forced him to relax his expression and confine his amazement to his voice. "Ouch! Damn it!" He rubbed at his forehead carefully avoiding contact with the wound. "You're kidding me? Christ, I bet Greg was surprised."

A mischievous glint shining in his eye, Dark said, "So I have been told."

"I'd like to have seen that." Connor smiled, imagining the way Greg must have looked when he found out Webb wasn't whom he had thought. Sobering, Connor glanced back at Dark's mangled body. "So then what happened?"

"Dr. Pierce, Mitch and the others went looking for you." Dark's voice cracked at the end of each sentence and Connor could tell the man was staying awake for his benefit. "A storm stalled them for a few days, but they tracked you down at the Dena'ina settlement far north of here."

Pulling the blanket higher against the chill in the room, Connor let his mind envision the bonding ceremony and the last time he saw his new lover. "That's Adam's tribe. I...I only met a few of them. I must have hit my head when I got thrown off the snow machine." He blinked to try and dispel the bright lights exploding behind his eyes, making them water. "Thank God I have a thick skull, considering how many times it's been cracked this week."

Connor glanced up at the hanging IV bottles and recognized one solution as a medication used to reduce swelling in the brain. "Mannitol. Looks like I gave Greg a few problems."

Grunting an affirmative sound, Dark shifted on the bed, groaning softly under his breath. "He was very worried. He said there was too much pressure on your brain. You only started getting better late last night."

Glancing up at the clock on the far wall, Connor closed his eyes and opened them again, but his distorted vision made the clock unreadable. "How long have I been back?"

"Just over a day." Dark gestured with his bandaged fingers at the empty chair beside Connor's bed. "Dr. Pierce or one of the others has been at your side nearly every minute since you got back. Even Mitch. Rose just left."

Dark huffed and settled back into the pillows, a pleased smirk on his lips. "I'm just happy you're back. It gives them someone else to fuss at and hover over all the time." He darted a glance at the empty doorway and lowered his voice conspiratorially. "They can be really annoying."

Returning the amused grin, Connor shared a moment of companionable silence with Dark, but his thoughts returned to Adam. He looked up to find Dark staring at him, as if he was waiting for something. Feeling like a young boy confessing to his father, Connor stuttered out his next question. "Ah, Dark? About the 'your mate' thing from before? I, well, I...."

Eyes filled with kindness, Dark stopped the embarrassed stammering. "You are a child of the moon, Connor. You bear its mark. It is your destiny to mate with the Dena'ina warrior. I have known of it since you arrived. He is a blessed guardian of the night and the spirits chose you for his mate."

"Marked? How?"

"Here and here." Dark gestured at his own face, touching the places where Connor bore scars on his cheek and over his eye, one shaped like a crescent and the other shaped like the native symbol for the moon.

"Your destiny was set in place from the moment you received your first marking. The moon has claimed you, just as your warrior has."

"Claimed me?" Connor blushed and tried not to duck his head, embarrassed the other man seemed to already know about his intimate relationship with Adam.

"Are you not bonded? Has he not given you his body and spirit, and taken yours to be his own?"

Connor squirmed and shifted his butt against the sheets, automatically clenching his ass at the memory of their long night of lovemaking. "Yes, he did. I never understood what it could be like until Adam. To give myself over completely, in every way. No wonder Greg was so hot to convince me to give in to him."

He looked sheepishly up at Dark, a deep blush on his pale cheeks. "But I'm glad I waited for Adam. He'll be the first and only."

"The first? The first one to what?" Greg stood in the open doorway to the room, dressing supplies piled in his hands and a suspicious look on his face. When Connor nervously darted his gaze away to look at anything but him, Greg appeared to instantly understand the implication.

"You let that guy, a *stranger*, do what you wouldn't let me even talk to you about?" Greg's indignant voice bounced off the stark walls. "I can't believe this! You must have hit your head harder than I thought the first time."

"Greg, I'm sorry," Connor sighed, then steadied his voice. "Please try and understand." His voice was firm, but his eyes still pleaded with Greg for understanding. "I'm... it was different with Adam. *I* feel different with Adam. He makes me feel...." His hands fisted the blanket until his knuckles turned white, "I don't know -- whole... finished. Like we're two interlocking halves of one soul."

Greg strode to Connor's bedside, his cheeks flushed and his lips forming a thin, straight line. "Isn't that just wonderful? Like a fairy tale romance. And after only a few days." He slammed the dressing supplies down onto the bedside table. "I've been trying to get you to *interlock* with me for five goddamned months!"

The loud slap of the equipment hitting the table made Connor cringe. He pressed a hand to his aching temple, inadvertently brushing against his new suture line.

"Ow! Son of a --," Connor yanked his hand up to automatically grab for the source of the stabbing pain. The sudden movement tugged one of his IV lines partially free, pulling tape and hair off his arm. "Shit! Damn it!"

"For Christ's sake, lie still!" Greg surged forward and grabbed Connor's arm, anchoring the loose IV line before it could pull out completely. Sitting down on the edge of the bed, Greg gently pried Connor's hand away from the wound.

Connor's torso twisted as his arm was pulled away. He cried out and clutched his chest. "Ow, augh! Christ, Greg! Watch it! My chest!"

The shouting and loud noises brought a new visitor into the room. An alarmed expression on his face, Mitch appeared in the doorway watching the two men grapple on the bed. Seemingly satisfied there wasn't a new crisis unfolding, he causally leaned against the doorjamb. He silently watched the two doctors, occasionally throwing an amused glance in Dark's direction.

Exasperated, Greg grabbed Connor's shoulders and yelled, "For God's sake, would you just hold still?"

When Connor relaxed, Greg settled comfortably on the bed and opened the top of Connor's hospital gown to reveal a moderate-sized, gauze dressing over Connor's left upper chest wall. Voice calmer, he muttered, "You got a couple of burns on your chest."

The guilty edge to Greg's tone made Connor look up from the wound to gaze at Greg's lowered head. "How? I don't remember any burns before."

Greg stayed silent for several beats, then sighed and looked up, a solemn, tired expression on his face. "When we found you, a black wolf-*thing* was attacking you."

A sharp cough from the direction of the doorway made Greg squirm. He threw a foul look at Mitch, but then quickly added, "Well, I *thought* it was attacking you. I drove my snow machine at it. You stumbled in the way and got thrown backward. You hit your head on a rock and some hot embers from the fire rolled into your shirt."

Connor paled and his voice shook. "What happened to the black wolf?" Greg didn't answer right away.

Emily entered the room, breaking the awkward silence that followed. A tiny, raven-haired woman in her mid-twenties, she easily slipped past Mitch's large frame and walked directly to Connor's bedside, a small, fluid-filled syringe in hand.

Greg glanced at her, then at the syringe. "Thanks, Emily. Perfect timing, I'm just about to change his dressing."

She gave Connor a tiny wave and huge grin of greeting, then stepped over to the IV poles, obviously not prepared to interrupt the conversation. Grabbing one of the IV lines, she injected the medication from her syringe into the tubing before Connor could comment.

Connor twisted his head slightly to follow Emily, but every movement, no matter how slight, gave him a pounding headache and intensified his nausea. He settled for giving Greg a puzzled look.

"It's just a sedative, something for the pain." Greg's voice dropped low, growing gentle and soothing. "You'll need it when I change the dressing." He slowly loosened the tape holding Connor's old bandage in place, alternating his gaze between the wound and Connor's face. "You know how burns hurt when the air hits them."

Emily finished injecting the medication, patted Connor on his uninjured shoulder and wordlessly left the room.

The dressing was removed and cool air hit the areas of red, raw, burned flesh on his chest. The first wave of pain struck. Connor hissed and tightly clenched his eyes shut, fingers twisting into the blankets. As Greg worked over the wound, the pain began to ease as the medication did its work.

"The wolf, Greg." Even through gritted teeth, Connor's voice wavered, but his pained glare was full of determination.

Heaving a sigh, Greg avoided looking at Connor, focusing on what his hands were doing instead. "I-I don't know. It got hit with the machine." He sighed again then hardened his tone. "It's probably dead. I didn't stay around long enough to be sure."

"Dead? He's dead? Why didn't you check?" An odd feeling of dread closed over Connor and panic swelled in his chest. If it was only a wolf, why did it matter? He couldn't remember what happened during the ceremony, but he was sure this was important. He glanced over at Dark and got nothing more than a sympathetic nod. Mitch's face held its usual calm, unperturbed expression.

Anger and resentment sparked in Greg's eyes and a tinge of red colored his cheeks. He stopped working and glared at Connor. "Because I was too busy trying to get your ungrateful *ass* some medical attention."

Feeling unjustly chastised, exhaustion tugged at Connor and he began to lose the urge to argue. Lowering his voice, Connor gripped one of Greg's wrists, gently stilling it. "It was my head that needed the attention, Greg." He gave the man a weak, exhausted smile.

Greg's lips twitched, but no smile surfaced. He lowered his own voice and muttered, "Oh that's right. Your ass got all the attention earlier."

Releasing his grip, Connor let his arm fall to the bed in defeat. "Christ, just let it go, Greg."

"I'll let it go, right along with you. No problem, if that's what you want." Greg stared at Connor and swallowed hard when the other man didn't contradict him. "Okay then. Get some rest." Greg dressed the wound, eyes never looking up from their task.

As the medication took greater effect, Connor slowly relaxed. Despite the foggy euphoric feeling invading his mind, he needed to know more. He ached for Adam to be at his side. "Where's Adam?"

Putting the last of the tape in place, Greg closed the gown, hesitating a moment to pick up and examine the silver band Mitch had insisted they leave around Connor's neck.

"There wasn't anyone left." Greg hurriedly dropped the band and pulled the blankets up higher over Connor. "They all disappeared during the ceremony we interrupted. There were only a pack of wolves there when we found you, no people."

"Adam would have come after me if he could have."

"Nobody stayed behind to protect you, Connor." Greg touched the side of Connor's face, lightly caressing it for a brief moment. "No one. You're deluding yourself if you believe some guy you met four days ago is going to risk his life for you and declare undying love."

172

Out There in the Night

Greg hurriedly gathered up the garbage from the dressing change and stood up. He stared down at Connor's stricken face and his tone softened, but a touch of anger still lingered in his eyes. "I wished it did, but it just doesn't happen that way in real life. Nobody's that devoted. Trust me. He left you alone with a great, big, black wolf at your throat."

Connor watched as Greg pointedly ignored the displeased glare on Mitch's face, pushing past him out into the hallway. Greg's heavy strides echoed down the hall before being cut off altogether by the slamming of a door.

Devastated, Connor turned his face away from the two men remaining in the room, hot tears streaking down his cheeks. His heart ached and in that moment, he suddenly knew he truly loved Adam, needed him. Greg was wrong. He had to be wrong.

A light touch on his shoulder jerked Connor back from his thoughts. He sniffed and clumsily wiped at his face before turning his head. Mitch crouched at his side, his dark eyes shining with a curious light, understanding and affection clearly written on the man's face.

"Do not believe everything you hear, young one. Dr. Pierce is not so experienced in the ways of true love as he thinks. Not yet. Open your heart and trust in what it tells you. Let the spirits guide you. They will lead you to the truth." Mitch patted his shoulder again, turned off the bedside lights and quietly left the room.

Connor closed his eyes and concentrated on listening to the feelings swirling around in his head and in his heart. They were a jumble of confused thoughts

173

and nightmarish visions. Shadows danced, drums beat, and people changed from human to furred beasts and back again. There was pain, pleasure and sizzling pulses of heat and burning desire, all mixed with the heavy, grounding sensation of a love so true and fierce Connor could not only feel it, but taste it and hear it, as well.

It all added up to one person, one being. As consciousness faded, he called out, the word echoing in his mind and the darkness of his room, pleading for the one thing that would make him whole again.

"Adam!"

**

On a ridge just north of town, Adam impatiently waited under the protective cloak of night. The waxing moon shone brightly through an ever-changing, cloud-speckled sky. Stars peeked out between the shadowed masses, and the air felt crisp and sharp to his sensitive nose.

In his alpha wolf form, Adam paced and pranced, restless and angry. He stopped, and raised his muzzle into the air, howling at the night. It was a long, low, mournful sound that bounced off the frozen hills. A chorus of sympathetic voices echoed the howl, their wolf song carrying on the rising winds.

Waiting on the fringes of the dense woods outside of Nekenano, Adam was growing increasingly tense.

Out of the woods trotted the old gray wolf, Dyami, the tribal medicine man, who quietly joined Adam. Dyami immediately transformed into a man.

Adam reluctantly did the same. Despite the
state, neither one felt the bitter cold.

Dyami laid a weathered hand on Adam's broad
shoulder. "Be at peace, Adam. The time to rejoin your
mate has not yet come."

Adam stared off into the night, eyes riveted on
the town lights a few miles below them. "My spirits
yearn for him, Dyami. Now that we have bonded, I am
not whole without him near."

Nodding, the shaman dropped his hand from
Adam's shoulder and pointed a crooked finger at
Adam's heart. "As it should be. He has the same
yearning, but he may not recognize the need for what it
is yet. He has to learn to accept it."

"When will that be, Dyami?" Adam frowned.

"When he comes to you of his own free will.
Then he will truly be yours, not because of the changes
the spiritwalkers have blessed him with, but because he
wants to be your mate."

"The full moon will be in two days. I cannot
wait two days to know he is all right."

"The re-injury to his head was harsh. He has
need of the white man's care and medicines for now."
Dyami looked to the sky and appeared to listen to the
winds blowing past him. "The spirit of Meachee is
watching over him, protecting him. His fate is in the
hands of his own people for now. You must wait for
him to heal and to accept his destiny."

"That is much to ask of a young outsider in such
a short time."

"He is capable. The ancients would not have
chosen him otherwise. He is no longer an outsider, he is

175

now your mate."

Adam drew in a deep breath and concentrated on touching Connor's spirits through their fledgling bond.

"Yes, he is strong." A feeling of warmth and joy coursed through Adam, his own soul thrilled by the discovery of Connor nearby. "Even now I can feel him." A bright, white thread Adam recognized as Connor's spirits touched his heart. He drew in the sensation and let his own spirit mingle with it.

A sudden burst of searing pain and loss flashed through Adam, and he heard Connor calling his name. His voice was weak and trembling with fear. Adam could feel the isolation, despair and loneliness his mate was feeling across their spiritual connection just as plainly as if the pain was his own.

Tormented by the idea Connor was in great distress, Adam instinctively morphed into his more powerful, faster werewolf form. Ignoring Dyami's warnings and pleas, intent only on protecting and comforting his injured mate, Adam bounded off, racing toward Nekenano.

***

A lone wolf howled in the distance, the eerie sound echoed by several more mournful voices on the winds. Greg shifted restlessly in his chair at the foot of Connor's bed and glanced at Mitch.

The guide was framed in the doorway, his broad back pressed against the jamb to support his weight. His smooth, ageless face looked pensive and distant to

Greg. Both men were tired, but neither could find any rest tonight. Within an hour of turning in, they both found themselves at Connor's bedside keeping vigil.

Greg slumped his tall frame down deeper into the cushions of the chair and stared at the bruised and bandaged face of his friend. Every few minutes his gaze darted to the bedside monitor and various IV tubings, checking that things were all right and Connor was stable.

Mitch seemed frozen in place by the door. The barest movement of his chest and the slow blinking of his eyes were the only signs he hadn't fallen asleep standing up.

Even through they hadn't spoken since entering the room, Mitch's presence gave Greg comfort. Rolling his head across the back of the chair seat, Greg sighed and closed his eyes, soothing the irritated burning making them feel raw and blurry. Surprisingly, he felt more secure slouched in the uncomfortable small chair at the foot of Connor's bed then he had in his own room. Sleep began to pull at him and he felt the heaviness of unconsciousness begin to overtake his exhausted mind and body.

From somewhere in the back of the lodge, the harsh crash of breaking glass shattered the calm of the night. The chorus of mournful howling outside suddenly picked up. The winds rustled, rattling the shingles on the roof and rapped hard against the thick windowpanes.

Startled, both Mitch and Greg jerked upright, trading bewildered stares.

Jumping up from the chair, Greg rubbed at his

burning eyes. "What the hell was that? A window?"
He quickly ran a clinical eye over both Connor and
Dark, not surprised both medicated men were
undisturbed by the loud crash.

Mitch looked down the hallway in the direction
of the sound and shrugged. "Winds might have put a
tree limb through one. From that old pine on the back
side of the lodge. I'll go check."

In two long strides Greg was at Mitch's side.
"I'm coming with you. We've had plenty of high winds
before and that tree has never lost a needle, let alone a
branch big enough to break a window. I'm getting a
rifle first, too, just in case the beast that was after
Connor has come looking for him."

Mitch shrugged again and quietly reassured
Greg. "There was no beast. They were ceremonial
headdresses and skins. It was a trick of the firelight."

Greg sniffed and rubbed his eyes again,
exhaustion and sarcasm heavy in his voice. "Yeah sure,
and you don't listen to the wind talk to you, either."

The sound of more glass breaking interrupted
Mitch's response and he took off down the hall, Greg
matching him stride for stride.

Within moments, Adam loped into the
unguarded ward from the other end of the hallway and
headed straight to Connor's side. In full werewolf form,
Adam towered over the bed, dwarfing the sleeping
man.

Easing his massive bulk onto the mattress,
Adam leaned down to sniff and nuzzle at Connor's
neck, as if to reassure himself his mate was well.
Pushing the dressings aside, he licked at the wound on

Connor's forehead, and then worked his tongue down over the man's neck and chest. Finding the fresh burn, he removed the gauze with a gentle paw and lavished the blistered flesh with several strokes of his tongue.

A flash of pain crossed Connor's face as he slowly began to surface from the depths of a drugged sleep. Looking up through mere slits, unable to move his head off the pillow to get a better look, Connor blinked hard and tried to open his eyes wider. The awesome creature from his dreams materialized a few scant inches from his face. A burst of excitement and fear lanced through him.

The beast tilted its head to one side and a beam of moonlight from the window was caught by something in the animal's thick, dark fur.

Connor's expression relaxed, as fear melted into the comforting glow of recognition. Barely able to lift his hand, Connor reached out and touched the silver band braided into the black fur. His fingertips grazed it before falling back to the mattress, the heavy pull of the drugs dragging him back down toward sleep.

"Adam?" Connor smiled as his eyes fell shut, then he repeated the plea with more confidence and understanding. "Adam."

Responding to Connor, Adam instantly shifted from skinwalker to his naked human form. Finding the silver band still tied around the doctor's neck, he moved it over Connor's heart and placed a gentle kiss on his mate's chest through the band. He was still leaning over, lips pressed tightly to his lover when Mitch and Greg tore back into the room.

"Get the hell away from him!" Greg yelled from

the doorway. He pulled up his rifle, aiming it at Adam, but hesitated a second, distracted by the intruder's total naked state.

"Wait! You're too close. You might hit the boy!" Mitch knocked the rifle barrel up into the air as the gun fired, shattering one of the fluorescent lights in the ceiling. The gunfire shocked Greg, freezing him in place, a stricken expression on his face.

Adam rose up off the bed and stood staring at his limp, battered mate, his dark eyes roving over the IVs and medical equipment Connor was connected to. He turned to face the other men full on, and cast a hard glare at Greg.

Even through visibly intimidated, Greg's gaze was still drawn to the impressively large and fully erect cock bobbing against Adam's hard-packed abdomen. He had a sudden understanding why Connor had developed an attraction for this massive, wild man.

Sniffing the air once again, Adam cocked his head in Mitch's direction, then nodded once, apparently arriving at some decision. With one last lingering gaze at Connor, Adam cleared Connor's bed in one powerful leap and plunged out one of the three windows lining the wall of the wardroom. Glass littered the room and tumbled out into the night. In seconds, the darkness had swallowed Adam, leaving a slack-mouthed Greg, an awestruck Dark, and a silent Mitch staring after him.

***

Sitting on the floor by the bedroom door, Greg watched Mitch nail the last board into place over the broken window, locking out the last remaining draft in the room. He was surprised when his eyes strayed to the guide's bulging biceps, admiring the way the soft folds of his shirt strained against the taut fabric as Mitch worked.

The shirt pulled tight across his broad shoulders, his build more noticeable than usual with his long, shiny hair held back in a ponytail. The sway and dip of the thick, black hair down his back drew Greg's eyes lower. He was admiring the curve of Mitch's tight buttocks and the thickness of his thighs just as the guide turned around, his job complete.

Sighing at the loss of the newly discovered scenery, Greg licked his lips and blew out a deep breath to refocus his thoughts on the problems at hand. All his good intentions disappeared like smoke when Mitch dropped down on the floor beside him, sitting close enough their shoulders and thighs touched.

Mitch leaned forward and wrapped his arms around his bent knees, drawing Greg's eyes back to the well-defined muscles of his arms.

As he explored the other man with hungry eyes, Greg's gaze darted up to catch Mitch watching him. Chuckling nervously, he nodded at Mitch's shoulders. "I never noticed how muscular your arms were before. You work out?"

"I run."

Greg ran his eyes admiringly over Mitch's buff form again. "That explains the thighs, but running won't give you those kind of arms, my friend."

"I have my own style." Mitch sat back against the wall. "Gives your whole body a workout."

"Really?" Greg's eyebrows arched toward his well-groomed hairline. "I'd like to see that." He flexed his own lean arms, working the muscles of his upper limbs. "I could use a better workout. The last few days have shown me that much."

"If you want, I could teach you."

"Yeah? When?" Greg looked over at the far bed. After listening to Connor talk about how he felt about Adam, he knew their five-month relationship as lovers was over. He was sad, but he accepted it. Life was full of changes. "I think I'll have a lot of free time on my hands from now on."

"Then when Dr. Jacy is healed," Mitch turned and looked Greg directly in the eye, a spark of something Greg thought looked possessive and feral shining through, "I will take you." Then he winked at Greg. "Soon. Very soon, you will run with me."

***

Chapter Thirteen

Connor slept all night and most of the next day. Repeated head injuries, pain medications, sheer exhaustion and the mounting stress of the sudden, unexpected changes in his life had drained him to his lowest point of tolerance.

Slowly getting his bearings, the sound of heavy, regular breathing drew Connor's attention to the chair by the door where Mitch sat, feet propped up on a stool, fast asleep. Connor flashed a look at the other guide. Dark was awake, but silent in his own bed.

Seeing less tubes and wires running from the older man, Connor breathed a sigh of relief. Even the chest tube was gone. Connor sat up in bed without any obvious difficulty and Dark's mouth pulled into a thin-lipped smile of sincere pleasure.

"You are feeling better. I am pleased. The spirits continue to watch over you. You are much blessed in the spirit world. Your two spirits make you very powerful."

"Two spirits." Connor rubbed lightly around the bandage on his chest, remembering the way Adam had touched his heart when he talked about Connor being a two spirit. "That's what Adam called me. He made it sound important."

His chest ached and he knew it was from more than just the burn on his skin. He ached for the sound and feel of Adam, wanting, needing him to be close.

Voice rough with disuse and age, Dark rumbled,

"It is what allows you to love a man as you would a woman. Both spirits of man and woman dwell within your soul. You were born a two spirit. You will always be a two spirit and that gives you strength. Strength you will need, to accept the changes in your life that are coming."

"This is all too confusing." Raising the head of the bed with the remote control, Connor sighed and lay back against the pillow. Pulling the covers up higher against the non-existent chill, he sank into the feeling of warmth and comfort the cocoon of blankets gave him.

"I like my life." One hand automatically went to his forehead and Connor rubbed at the only undamaged skin he found, trying to soothe away the riot of emotions and confusing memories flooding his mind. "I don't want to give it up."

"You are happy here with Dr. Pierce as your mate? You are content to be with him for all time?"

Blushing a bit, Connor glanced at the closed door to the room. "Well, no, not exactly." He sighed again and slumped deeper into his protective cocoon. "I mean, Greg is a great guy, a good friend, and a terrific doctor, but," he rolled his head on the pillow and looked out the window in the direction he thought the Dena'ina settlement would be, "I'm not in love with Greg. And Greg's not in love with me."

His eyes watered and his voice caught on the words. "I didn't realize how much I was missing out on until these last couple of days." He glanced over at Dark. "With Adam. I really miss him. I don't know what he is, but I miss him."

Dark's voice grew stronger and more

demanding. "You do not know *what* he is?"

His harsh tone made Connor sit up straighter. "I know what I saw, what I *think* I saw. I'm just having trouble believing it."

Connor darted a wide-eyed, frightened look at the waiting man. "Adam's more than just a man. He's part… something else… part animal."

The faint pulsing beat of the ceremonial drums began pounding in his head in time with the light throbbing of his headache. Connor absently pulled the covers closer, and tried unsuccessfully to push the rhythm from his mind.

"You know what word to use, young one. Say it."

Shaking his head slightly to dislodge the sound of the drums, Connor grimaced when the soft litany of now-familiar native chanting joined the music. The primal rhythm grew louder and visions from the last few days raced through his mind. Flashes of making love with Adam were mixed with visions of an orange-eyed, black wolf. All of them merging and blending until Adam and the wolf were one and the same.

Connor gasped and clenched his eyes shut, fighting the onslaught of memories, fear and excitement battling for dominance in his heart. The soothing soft tones of a flute joined the pounding beat of the drums, and the chanting became a whisper, light and muted.

Something deep inside of Connor stirred to life and his fear melted away. A yearning to be with his new mate rose to the surface and blotted out everything else. Connor realized he was in love, in love with a supernatural creature.

185

"Werewolf. Adam's a werewolf." The moment he said the word aloud a sense of peace and acceptance descended on Connor, leaving him feeling protected and happier than he had ever felt before in his life. He stared out the window that separated him from the outside world and longed for the gap between him and where he needed to be to magically disappear.

"Yes, he is." Dark's tone was just as stern and demanding as before, but now it carried a note of pride and satisfaction. "What else does that mean? For you?"

Bits and pieces of past conversations about the native myths and legends over the last few months tumbled together with things Adam had tried to explain in his abbreviated, cryptic manner. Suddenly, the truth crystallized in Connor's thoughts. He paled as the solid weight of the knowledge hurtled down on him full force.

"I'm a werewolf, too. He made me a werewolf." Panic set in and Connor's feelings of protection and safety faltered. He sat up in bed, dropping the covers and felt his face, searching for changes in his appearance. Pulling open his gown, he checked his chest, but found only the burn dressing, which he frantically pulled off to look under. "Adam made love to me and changed me into a *monster*."

"You think Adam is a monster?"

Dark's deep, commanding voice shot out of the darkness and drove a spike of dread through Connor's heart, stilling his actions and halting his frantic thoughts.

Was Adam a monster? He had rescued Connor when he would have certainly died in the freezing

186

wilderness without help. Then he cared for him, nursing him back to health, held him while he vomited endless times and cleaned him up afterwards. Not many men Connor knew would have done that for him. No, Adam wasn't a monster.

"I-I... there is so much I'll have to leave behind. Everything I've worked for all my life, my family, friends, my medical practice, even my place back home."

"You were destined to this fate, Connor." Dark's tone was firm, full of wisdom and conviction. "The moon has chosen you, just as she chose Adam. She chooses all of her guardians. To be a skinwalker, a werewolf, is a great blessing from the spiritwalkers."

"So I'm supposed to give up my entire life because some spirit world has decided to give me away to some mythical werewolf creature?" Connor's voice trembled, his face paler than usual.

"The moon picked you, but Adam loves you. He would not have mated with you if he did not. Not even the power of the moon could convince him to take a mate for all time he did not love. Do you love him?" Demanding an answer, the older man's voice surged with a sudden power and authority Connor knew he had to respond to.

"Yes, damn it, I do. More than I thought I could love another person." Tears welled up in his eyes, but Connor refused to allow them to fall. "Except he's not just a regular person, now is he?"

"No. So you must ask yourself, is it too much to give up for eternal love?"

Adam had protected him, cared for him, even

courted him in his own unusual fashion with conversation, gentle touches, gifts and declarations of undying love and loyalty. Adam had been assertive and unwavering in his absolute certainty they had been meant for one another. He was the first and only man with whom Connor had felt comfortable enough to have intercourse, a truly unexpected event in Connor's mind. He'd shown Connor everything the young doctor had ever dreamed of finding in a life partner. Connor only had one reservation left.

"I can't stop being a doctor."

"A medicine man is always a blessing to a tribe, Connor. Adam will teach you what you need to know to exist in both the human and the spirit worlds. He has managed both for one hundred years."

"One hundred years? God, I always knew I'd marry an older man." Connor smiled shyly and quipped, "Damn good thing he's kept his figure."

Dark softly snorted. "One hundred years of running as alpha in a pack of wolves and skinwalkers will keep anyone fit. You will see for yourself in time."

Connor started, nervously picking at the edges of the healing, odd-shaped burn over his heart. "This is a hard decision to make. It's the rest of my life. There's no going back after this."

Dark hammered home the reality of the situation one more time. "You have already been chosen, young one. The only decision left to make is whether you will live with or without your mate. But make no mistake, after the full moon tomorrow night, you will be a part of the spirit world, a blessed guardian of the night. You will run as one with the other skinwalkers on this earth.

The great spirits have already bestowed their blessing on you. There is no going back *now*."

The door to the ward opened and Mitch slipped quietly in. He sat down in the chair by the door, obviously planning on spending the night on guard against any more unexpected, late night visitors. Mitch nodded a wordless greeting to Connor.

Connor didn't return the greeting, but he caught Mitch trade a sharp glance and a head shake with Dark before he settled more comfortably in his chair and began looking through a hunting magazine.

Confused and exhausted, Connor lowered the bed and slipped down under the covers before turning out the small over bed light with the pull string.

The moment the light went out a lonesome, anguished howl came from the direction of the thick woods just beyond the town.

He immediately knew it was Adam calling to him. A lump formed in Connor's throat and the ache in his chest grew until he thought his heart would burst.

Through all his confused and jumbled thoughts, the knowledge he truly and deeply loved Adam was the one thing that never changed. Despite all his fears and uncertainties, that feeling of deep, abiding love never faltered. Connor knew, no matter what Adam was, no matter what the future held, he needed to be with his mate.

***

After lying awake watching Mitch read for hours, Connor felt strangely refreshed. Halfway through the night, Greg had relieved the guide. The dark-haired doctor was now sleeping in the chair, dark head and chiseled chin resting on his chest. The sound of his soft snoring set a regular tempo in the otherwise silent room.

Connor knew from experience, Greg only snored when he was exhausted and deeply asleep. He took advantage of the moment, quietly slipping out of the bed. Gait wobbly and head still aching, he searched the closet for something to wear, and found his boots and the ceremonial buckskins Adam had given him. He pulled on the simple clothes and stepped into the boots, ignoring the absence of socks or underwear.

The sound of a drawer sliding open, followed by the tiny rattle of keys startled him. Connor spun around to face the source of the noise, and found he needed to grip the corner of the closet door to keep his balance. Moving with exaggerated care, Connor walked to Dark's bedside and caught the key ring the old guide tossed at him.

"The brass one opens the shed behind my place. Take the old red snow machine on the left. It's seen better days, but it will take you to where you need to be."

Dark's voice was once again the coarse, rusty whisper Connor had grown to recognize over the months he spent in the old man's company. It had been time well-spent learning about the people here, and about himself as well, through the eyes of a man he had grown to think of as a good friend and a father figure.

"Thanks," Connor whispered back warmly. "I don't think I can make it on my own." He stepped closer, recovering from a small stumble as he did. "Still a little unsteady, it seems."

He smiled at Dark and grasped his arm. Squeezing it, he tried to let his eyes and his touch tell the man how much he appreciated the offer and the months of his friendship.

"Thanks for everything, Dark. I'm sure even I don't know how much I'm going to appreciate everything you've given me since I've been here." He let go of the man's arm and made his way around the bed toward the door and the sleeping figure in the chair. "I'll let Adam teach me how much that really is, and come and tell you myself when I can."

Dark winked at him and nodded at the door. "Learn well and make me proud. Travel light and take the old parka that hangs on the hook inside of the shed. With the hood up, no one will recognize you when you leave town."

Edging closer to the door and Greg, Connor stopped and tilted his head toward his ex-lover. "Tell Greg I knew he'd understand."

He smiled and waved, then slipped out into the hallway, glad it wasn't Mitch standing guard. Mitch never seemed to sleep when he was watching over them and Connor knew he would never have made it past the experienced, sharp-eyed guide.

Using the wall to steady himself, he made his way through the dimly lit corridor, out into the cold reception room then through the double doors and into the deserted kitchen of the lodge. He took a moment to rest and congratulate himself for his stealthy escape, and then Connor slipped up the back stairs and into his room. He grabbed a few personal belongings that were especially important to him and stuffed everything into a small knapsack.

A snapshot of a smiling Greg embracing him stared back at Connor from the nightstand. Connor hesitated, then sat down on the bed, pulling a tablet and a pen off the bedside table. He scribbled a quick note and left it in the middle of the bed. Grabbing his back-up parka out of the closet, he made his way back downstairs and into the lodge kitchen.

Taking a deep breath, he bit his lower lip then walked out the back door, slipping into the pre-dawn darkness.

It took Connor twice as long as usual to get to Dark's place only a few blocks away. He had to stop frequently and rest, hiding behind buildings and watching for the early risers in town. He didn't want to risk another rescue party forming before he even left town.

Inside the shed, he found both the parka and the snow machine right where Dark said they would be. The parka was old and two sizes too big, but it covered him from his head to his knees and left room for him to keep his own coat on, as well.

The snow machine started without problems. Connor eased it out of the shed, stopping only to close and lock the door behind him. He took the shortest route out of town, even waving at Joss as the man walked into the sheriff's office from his truck. Joss absent-mindedly waved back.

Once Connor reached the ridge leading to the woods where Adam had spent the night calling to him, he let the engine loose and made a break for the woods. Within seconds a dark, supple shape flashed by him. As it circled around and came up beside him to run at his side, the shape became distinguishable as a huge, black wolf.

Connor gleefully laughed at the bared teeth the wolf showed him and took off after the beast as it surged in front of him, leading the way home.

***

Chapter Fourteen

The warmth of the hand gripping his shoulder seeped into Greg's exhausted brain faster than the shaking motion woke up his body. He opened his eyes to see Mitch's expressionless face. The guide knelt beside the chair where Greg had fallen asleep.

Greg looked around the room. Dark's eyes were closed and he was breathing softly, his casted arm rising and falling with each shallow inspiration. Morning light filtered through the intact windows and illuminated the empty, rumpled bed where Connor had been sleeping.

"Where is he?" Startled, his stomach knotted in fear, Greg pushed to his feet, looking wildly around the room.

"Gone." Mitch rose to his feet and blocked the doorway. "I checked his room. His backpack is gone and so are some of his clothes and personal things. Wherever he went, he went under his own power, willingly."

Greg pushed past Mitch and raced out of the room. "You don't know that. He has a head injury. He isn't making sound decisions. We have to go after him."

He ran in long determined strides, but was outdistanced by the quicker man. Mitch stopped him in the middle of the lodge's cozy living room.

"The decision is Dr. Jacy's to make, Greg, not yours."

194

"I know, but he's not well." Greg tried to move past the broader man, then hesitated, a slight frown burrowing his forehead. "Did you just call me 'Greg'? You've never called me 'Greg'. Not once in three years."

Mitch nodded and began unbuttoning his shirt. "Now, it is fitting that we call each other by our given names."

He slowly advanced on the flustered doctor, forcing Greg to walk backwards, deeper into the room.

Licking his lips, Greg watched Mitch's hands slide the shirt off, revealing a rock-hard chest and tapered waist, covered with unblemished, dark crimson skin. He fought to keep the slight stammer out of his voice.

"Now? Why now?"

The predatory look in Mitch's eyes both excited and unnerved Greg. He stumbled a little, knocking into a small side table. He hastened to grab the carved box tumbling off the top. By the time he had replaced it and looked back up, Mitch was completely undressed, directly in front of him. Naked and hard, and as always, waiting.

Eyes drawn downward, Greg let the tip of his tongue escape his parted lips, impressed by the man's natural attributes. Mitch's cock stood out from his body, slightly curved, thick at the base, and long. It was dark, lined with bulging veins, the taut, uncut foreskin tightly hugging the large head. Under Greg's appreciative scrutiny, the shaft bobbed and thickened even more. Greg's eyes widened and he bit down on the tip of his tongue. His gaze remained riveted to

Mitch's cock as he talked.

"Between you and the big guy from earlier, I'm beginning to see why those long, tall," Greg cocked his head from side to side, visually examining Mitch as best he could from a distance, "heavy totem poles are a symbol of your people."

He was startled out of his admiring stare by strong hands on his chest. "Hey! Don't you want to talk about this?"

Mitch closed the few feet between them and grabbed Greg by the front of his shirt. He yanked him forward, fingers busily unbuttoning and tugging the fabric from Greg's body.

Greg sputtered and chattered nervously, but didn't resist. "Isn't this a little sudden? I mean, really, you've never shown the least bit of interest in me before this. Mitch?"

"Sudden? No. I have waited for three years, Greg." Successfully removing Greg's shirt, Mitch's nimble fingers began working on the doctor's jeans and underwear. He had them hanging around Greg's knees in seconds. "Three long years."

With one good shove, Mitch dumped Greg onto the bearskin rug in front of the fire, his own body weight pinning the stunned man in place.

"But you never...I never...I didn't know...." Greg's half-hearted protests were cut off as Mitch sealed his mouth over Greg's still-muttering lips.

The kiss was deep, fierce and consuming. It turned Greg's spine to jelly, temporarily slowing his nervous babbling. By the time Mitch let him up for air, Greg was breathless, flushed and hard. He wanted more. His mouth had been thoroughly ravaged, and he couldn't help wondering how that talented tongue would feel on the rest of his body.

"Christ, Mitch, why've you only been using that mouth to talk with all these years?" He panted between words to try and slow his pounding heartbeat.

Moving swiftly, Mitch pulled back and pushed Greg's legs up and around his own waist, angling his hips just so.

Greg heard a sound he recognized as lube on skin and his eyes popped open wider as Mitch's hot slippery hand encased his straining cock. Two strokes later and Greg forgot about everything else, arching up into the tight heat of the man's fist.

"I have been waiting for your guilt and your heart to be free. Now I claim what has always been destined to be mine." With one forceful thrust, Mitch entered Greg, sliding his slick shaft to the root, grazing Greg's prostate in the forward lunge.

Face contorted in a mask of pleasure/pain, Greg gasped, and went rigid as a burst of white-hot passion sizzled up his spine and exploded behind his tightly clenched eyes.

"I should point out," Greg stammered, "I'm usually the one on top." Then he gasped and bucked his hips, seeking more of the wildly euphoric stimulation, despite his claim.

"Then I guess you have some adjusting to do." Mitch growled and thrust again, striking the sensitive nub on both strokes.

"Ah, well, I... shit... okay. Do that again."

Mitch smiled at the doctor's submissive

response.

Greg lost the ability to think straight as the head of Mitch's large shaft massaged his prostate over and over, sending a series of electric pulses through his body. Just as the rush of orgasm began to build deep in his balls and spine, the forceful thrusting action suddenly stopped.

Prying open his eyes, Greg saw Mitch poised motionlessly over him, expression soft and gentle, eyes exploring Greg's own face, as if reading his desire, gauging his reactions. Mitch's tender look was a contrast to the demanding physical ravishment. It unnerved Greg and took him by surprise.

"What? What's wrong?" Greg's body ached, teetering on the brink of explosion, held motionless by the sheer physical power of his lover and a tight stroking hand on his eager cock.

Mitch used a palm to forced Greg to look him in the eye. "Nothing's wrong. I just want to make sure your consent is given freely before we continue."

"What! You need consent *now*?" Greg squirmed his hips, clenching the muscles of his ass to convince Mitch to begin moving again. When that didn't work, he sighed and stared the quietly waiting man in the eye.

"Okay, okay. I consent!" He strained against Mitch's sweat-covered body and surged upward to lick the salty moisture from the man's neck, growling in Mitch's ear, "Move already! You want me so bad, then take me!"

He fell back down on the bearskin rug, his body vibrating beneath the relentless rhythm of Mitch's pounding thrusts. His orgasm came rushing back up, igniting a hailstorm of bright lights and heavy pressure in his head.

Just as the surge of power crackling through his body began to fade, Greg felt a strange pressure growing at the opening to his ass. He was still impaled on Mitch's rock-hard shaft despite the fact he had felt the spray of hot cum from the man bathe his inner walls during his own climax. Greg was surprised and pleased.

"Three years and I never knew you wanted me."

He gazed at Mitch's rugged face, then lowered his eyes to admire the bulging muscles of his shoulders and upper arms, running his hands over dips and curves of Mitch's back before dropping one hand to his own reviving cock. "I should have consented before this. Jesus! Go ahead, claim me, Mitch."

"I think I'll have to remind you of those words later." Mitch didn't give Greg time to question him before he began thrusting again, pulling him closer this time to whisper in his ear, "You'll have to learn to say my name properly from now on, as well."

Greg groaned bucking up into the thrusts, grunting out a strained, confused, "It's not 'Mitch'?"

Changing the angle of his penetration, Mitch slowed down his thrusts, teasing the head of his cock back and forth over Greg's sensitive prostate again and again until Greg was literally vibrating with extended pleasure. He brought his lips close enough to touch Greg's, then whispered into his panting mouth. "You say it wrong."

"I do?" Greg grabbed hold of Mitch's tense upper arms and dug his fingers into the hard muscles, a grimace of delirious lust and pain/pleasure on his handsome face. "How," he gasped and panted, "how should I say it?" He grunted out the last through clenched teeth as he teetered on the edge of a roaring climax.

"Me-AHT-chae. You pronounce it Me-AHT-chae."

"Okay, I-I got it. Me-AHT-chae." Greg bucked and wiggled in time to Mitch's soft words. "More hip and less lip here, please, Meachee."

Grunting out an amused chuckle, Mitch increased his tempo and pounded brutally into his new lover. He forced Greg over the edge of pleasure into a blinding climax that gripped the man so hard Mitch groaned from the tight spasms in Greg's ass. The rippling sensation of the rings of hidden muscle in Greg's body milked Mitch's shaft, wringing a climax from him and causing the base of his cock to swell and harden even more until they were completely locked together.

The growing pressure in his ass made Greg grunt aloud as the mixture of pain and delight burned in his ass. Exhausted and drained, he forced open his eyes, knowing he wore a sated, fucked-senseless expression on his face.

Above him, Mitch stared down at him with a tender expression of tolerant amusement on his lips. The expression miffed Greg a bit, but something else in Mitch's face drew his attention away from his wounded pride. His tongue felt thick, making it difficult to form his words, and his mind was still lazing about in a post-coital haze, but Greg just had to ask.

"I know I haven't been paying much attention to you until now, but your eyes haven't always been yellow, have they."

It was a statement. Greg was fairly certain this was a new development. Ego overcame the touch of fear the sight gave him and he smugly asked, "Did I just do that to you?"

A low growl and a deep, ravaging kiss was Mitch's only reply. It was going to be a very long and eventful night.

***

Chapter Fifteen

The trip to the cabin was exhilarating for Connor. The air was crisp and cold. The pre-dawn sky had been clear and bright, with twinkling stars and a shadow of the full moon due to peak that night. Even the usually sharp, biting winds had quieted to a gentle buffeting at his back, as if urging him along on his journey.

Alternating between running at his side and leading the way, Adam, in wolf form, had howled and yipped most of the trip. He occasionally came close enough to playfully nip at Connor's leg or tug at his sleeve.

Feeling oddly free, Connor's mood lifted and his sense of well-being skyrocketed. His headache didn't disappear, but the pounding in his temples had eased and the constant queasiness in his stomach melted away. His life was changing forever, going down a path he would never had foreseen or chosen on his own, but he accepted it, even looked forward to it as long as Adam was by his side.

Reaching the sturdy little cabin took time and skill. The valley was well hidden and surrounded by rugged, dangerous terrain. It was no wonder the settlement was so isolated. It was the perfect place for Adam's tribe. Not many outsiders would venture here without reason.

Parking the snow machine on the protected side of the cabin, Connor made his way into the warmth of the sheltering lodge, feeling as if he was finally home.

Still in wolf form, Adam followed closely behind Connor, but as he walked through the door, Connor's waist was enveloped in a pair of brawny, naked, human arms. The door closed behind them with a bang and a hot wet mouth descended on a patch of exposed skin at his neck.

"God, Adam! It feels so good to have you near me." Connor relaxed back into the man's embrace and let him do as he wanted with him, lost in the tingling sensations Adam was creating with his mouth at Connor's neck and ear.

Voice rough but tender, Adam whispered into Connor's wet ear, letting his lips brush against the sensitive outer shell as he spoke. "You will never leave me again, adada. I am not whole without you by my side."

Adam's arms moved lightning quick and his sure hands began stripping away the outer layer of Connor's clothing. Once Connor was wearing only the elk-hide pants and his boots, Adam caressed and stroked Connor's chest. His fingers explored the new burn on Connor's otherwise smooth chest, the touch delicate and caring. He traced the outline with one fingertip, then pulled Connor around to face him. Adam rained soft kisses down his lover's neck, trailing across to the burn over Connor's heart. Crouching slightly, he lightly licked the wounds again and again, coating them with saliva.

The warmth of the room seemed to rocket higher for Connor. He swayed slightly and broke out in a fine sheen of sweat. Eyeing the robust fire in the hearth, Connor chuckled breathlessly, running the fingers of one hand restlessly through Adam's long hair. "I see you kept the home fires burning. You knew I was coming?"

Never pausing, Adam murmured, "The winds told me. I wanted you to be comfortable without these." He released the ties to Connor's pants and let them drop to the floor around Connor's ankles. His hands slid lower to knead the firm muscles of Connor's ass, drawing a gasp from the doctor.

The rough texture of Adam's tongue against the healing flesh made Connor hiss and squirm, but after the first few strokes the sensation became pleasant, seductive even. His hands gripped Adam's thick upper arms for support. Oddly excited by the nurturing, decidedly canine act, Connor dropped his head to watch.

Each long, gentle swipe of Adam's flat, broad tongue over the newly forming scars left a glistening, wet trail behind. Connor's eyes followed each stroke. The rough touch and moist sounds caused his eager cock to stir. It filled and grew heavy, jutting out to poke against Adam's body.

The instant his cock touched Adam's heated flesh, a dam of pent-up desires flooded through Connor. He pulled Adam away from his chest and brought him up for a kiss. He hesitated, surprised by finding the silver band still strung around his own neck locked between Adam's lips.

Connor's heart swelled and he felt a shiver run down his spine when the big man pulled him closer and took the band from his mouth to sweetly kiss it before allowing it to swing back down to hang against Connor's wet chest. Adam's hands soothed the length of Connor's back and buttocks.

"What was that for?" Connor's voice trembled and his eyes grew damp at the adoring manner his lover handled both the band and his body.

Smiling, Adam murmured in Connor's ear. "We are bonded in the Dena'ina way, but we have yet to seal our joining with a kiss according to your white man's tradition. I thought I would start with the symbol of our love, in case you were feeling shy." The tone sounded closer to amusement than a virtuous declaration to Connor.

"I guess this is kind of like our wedding night."

In one frenzied motion, Connor pulled Adam's mouth down and sealed their lips together in a hot, demanding, explorative kiss that left them both panting for air.

But suddenly Connor pushed back from Adam. "Wait! Wait a minute!"

He backed away to stand panting in the middle of the room. Hurriedly grabbing his pants up from around his ankles, he eased them over his straining erection and held them securely in place. One hand outstretched in front of him, he silently stopped Adam from approaching him.

"We need to talk about some things first." Connor looked into the fire and lowered his voice, nervous over the tremor in his words. "I did a lot of thinking over the last two days. Dark… you know he's still alive, right?"

He stole a brief glance up at Adam then looked

back into the fire, afraid just looking at the man would erode his resolve to say the things he thought needed to be said before they took their relationship any further.

At Adam's brief nod, Connor dropped his hand from the air between them and relaxed slightly. He gripped the waistband of his pants tightly with both hands, twisting the hide in his fingers until the knuckles turned white.

"Dark told me a little bit more about things. Told me my life was changed forever, whether I wanted it to be or not. Told me this was all a good thing, a blessing, a gift."

Connor swallowed hard and forced himself to look Adam in the eye. "Warned me, really. About you." He swallowed past the lump forming in his throat and stood up straighter, as if rising to meet a new challenge. "And about me."

Watching Adam closely, Connor let his gaze linger over every square inch of the naked, bronze/cinnamon-colored man, admiring each defined muscle and sinewy curve on his large and heavy frame. He couldn't help but admire and respond to the sexual attractiveness of the man, but this time he looked at Adam's impressive build with a clinical eye. He noted what muscle groups had developed in response to a hundred years of four-legged running, how lean the ratio of muscle to fat was, how tapered Adam's legs and how strong his hands were. The amount of power there was frightening, frightening but sensual, too.

Slowly Connor lifted his eyes to Adam's face and drank in the sharp features, tracing his high cheekbones and full lips with his gaze. Locking his own green eyes to Adam's piercing black ones, Connor licked his lips nervously and drew in a deep breath to force out the words he had been so reluctant to say out loud for fear they would give them some kind of power over him.

"You're a werewolf. And I'm going to be one, too, aren't I?" Connor's voice rose and his words spilled out faster and faster. "You made me one, when we made love that night. When we made love and you didn't kill me afterwards. You did this to me."

Adam never flinched, but his face gentled and he stepped a pace closer, as if to comfort Connor. "I am what I am, a Dena'ina skinwalker." He touched his chest with one massive hand. "I would never harm you, Connor. We are children of the moon, not mindless killers for pleasure or sexual need. Skinwalkers guard the earth at night. We are caretakers and protectors. We help keep nature in balance. You are why I waited for one hundred years for a mate. Waited for you, Connor, only for you. You are my soul. You are *my* balance."

A shiver tore through Connor. He felt his face flush and his half-mast cock harden again. Connor's breathing faltered, catching in his chest. "How did you know I'd come?"

"Many told me of you. The moon chose you. The spirit world brought you here. The winds guided me to you and the spiritwalkers joined our souls together." Adam reached out to stroke Connor's cheek, slowly decreasing the distance between them as he talked. "Many others had a hand in forming our true path, but make no mistake, adada, it is I who love you."

"I... I...." Unable to say what was in his heart as visions of Adam morphing from man to wolf to werewolf kept playing in his mind, Connor stammered and gasped, his forehead wrinkled and a pained frown marred his face.

Trailing his hand down Connor's cheek, Adam stood in front of Connor. He crouched down and eased Connor's boots and socks off, then tugged the loose pants gently from the man's white-knuckled grip. He helped Connor step out of the last of his clothes and then kicked them to one side.

Rising up, Adam wrapped his thick arms around Connor's slim waist. Calm eyes locked on Connor's slightly panicked ones, Adam lifted his mate up until Connor's feet were off the floor. In three graceful, quick strides he made it to the bed. Without releasing Connor, Adam dropped to the mattress, pinning the smaller man. He held most of his weight up on his arms that were planted on either side of his trapped mate.

"Tell me." Adam nuzzled at Connor's neck, lavishing long, hot laps of his tongue over the soft sensitive skin from the shoulder to Connor's ear. He tugged at the small ear lobe and moistened the outer shell with his lips, breathing hotly against it, repeating his request over and over, until Connor moaned and arched up into the insistent embrace. "Tell me."

"Love you. I–I love you!" Connor bucked his hips and twisted, grinding his straining cock up against Adam's hot groin. "It doesn't make any sense, but I do!" His shaft slid alongside and over Adam's thick rod, the movement aided by sweat and the smooth, satiny touch of his own stretched and taut flesh.

Adam's shaft felt heavy and coarse to Connor, the foreskin dense with multiple folds of skin that tapered down the length to end in a thicket of prickly, bristle-like hairs. The sensation of it rubbing over Connor's smooth, circumcised cock was electric, sending bolts of excitement to the base of Connor's spine. From there the buzz traveled up and branched out, sizzling over every nerve cell and fiber in his body.

Connor felt light-headed and short of breath. He struggled against Adam's hold. He didn't want to get away. He wanted to crawl inside of the big man and bury himself deep inside of Adam's soul and never come out again. Anything less wouldn't be enough for him from now on. He wanted it all, everything life with Adam had to offer, bizarre blessings from the spirit world and all.

"More. I want more of you, Adam. Give me everything, now." Connor ducked his head and bit Adam on the neck, worrying the meaty flesh with his teeth and teasing over the small wound with jabbing strokes of his wet tongue.

The bite pulled a growl from Adam and Connor was rewarded with a frenzy of urgent activity. Adam grabbed Connor's legs and threw them over his shoulders, pressing their leaking cocks together.

Resting a good portion of his weight in the crook of Connor's widespread crotch and his own forearms, Adam ground his hips down in a circular fashion. Fingers firmly laced through Connor's blond hair, his lips and tongue explored Connor's face and neck, kissing and licking in a non-stop display of hungry affection. He delivered a few of his own sharp nips along the way, each one pulling a gasped groan from his lover.

Clear fluid leaked from the tip of Adam's large cock and he used the viscous substance to lubricate his shaft, rubbing the head over Connor's skin and groin. He marked Connor with his scent, the satiny stroking of flesh over flesh stimulating the production of more fluid from his own unique shaft.

The foreskin of Adam's cock slid back and forth over Connor's length, massaging against the shaft and occasionally catching on the edge of its head, teasing the sensitive underside.

Connor felt as if his body and mind were in overload. His neck was bitten, eyelids kissed, earlobes sucked, and his mouth was explored, while the taut nubs of his nipples were tweaked and pinched. The lingering scent of iqemik hung in the air, tickling his nose and the warmth from the blazing fire made his skin hot and flushed. The slick slip-slide of cock against cock was a delicious torment added to complete the wild ravaging of his senses.

Just when Connor felt a climax building, Adam shifted and heaved upward, taking Connor's hips with him. When they hit the bed again, Connor was completely impaled on Adam's shaft.

"Christ, Adam!" Connor cried out as the unexpected sensation of total penetration hit him full force. "Fuck!"

Adam responded as if the exclamation was a request from his lover. "Yes, adada." He bit down harder on the flesh under his mouth and bucked his hips forward, forcing a strangled sound of pleasure from between Connor's clenched teeth.

Adam's cock slid smoothly inside, gliding on the slick fluids against the satiny, moist lining of Connor's eager channel. Connor's ass spasmed and clenched, feeling stretched and fuller than he remembered feeling the last time they had done this.

His ass muscles flared again as Adam pushed in deeper. The coarse foreskin bunched at the base of the stout shaft to rub enticingly at the exposed ring of sensitive muscle guarding the breached opening to his body. The bristles of hair at Adam's groin ground over the soft flesh of Connor's butt cheeks, adding a sharp tingle of mild burning to the act.

Connor became aware of a slow build-up of pressure inside his ass. The expanding thickness at the base of Adam's cock made each thrust more delicious than the last. His opening was forced wider and wider until it refused to expand any more and Adam's cock was locked inside Connor's ass.

Apparently undaunted by the change in his ability to withdraw, Adam continued to pound into Connor, stroking deeper and deeper into him.

Connor could feel the tip of the shaft buried in his abdomen. The swollen base of Adam's cock grazed Connor's prostate again and again in a rapid-fire rhythm which caused bright bursts of fiery pleasure to explode along his nerves.

Dropping his legs down to Adam's waist, Connor forced a hand between their sweat-covered bodies. He grabbed his cock and palmed over the leaking head. He felt the hot glow of a flush spread rapidly over his entire body as his need for release began to peak. Connor changed his hold and began roughly stroking his shaft.

Able to keep up the demanding rhythm of thrusts into Connor's ass without difficulty, Adam continued to ravage the rest of Connor's body with his hands and lips. He nuzzled at Connor's neck, sucked on his jaw and devoured his ripe, panting mouth with his own full, wet lips.

Connor's body didn't know which sensation to pay attention to first. A sudden sharp pinch and flick at one erect, hot nipple shot to the front of his awareness and his orgasm rocketed up from somewhere deep in his groin. It blasted across every nerve ending in his flesh until it finally exploded in his head.

"Shit! Augh, ah, ah! Ah!" Connor bucked and screamed, his skin fever-hot and coated in sweat. The words in his head blew apart like scrabbled magnetic letters on a child's play board, leaving him with fragmented thoughts and distorted visions tumbling around in his brain.

Several rapid, deep thrusts jarred Connor across the bed and then Adam stilled and arched back from him. A hot, seeping sensation burned in his ass.

Through half-lidded eyes, Connor panted and wallowed in his own blaze of orgasmic pleasure and watched Adam's face contort into a tight grimace of pain/pleasure. Connor's eyes followed the arch of Adam's rigid body, taking in the bulging muscles, sweat-drenched, perfect flesh, and handsome high-boned features, stunned by the man's animalistic grace and beauty.

Out There in the Night

Still lost in a cloud of post-coital haziness, feeling euphoric and mute, Connor used his hands to worship the man towering overtop of him, sliding them up and over Adam's chest and neck again and again.

Slowly Adam relaxed, lowering his body down onto Connor, withdrawing his shrinking cock in small increments until it popped out of Connor's fluttering hole. Connor's arms and legs fell to the bed in an exhausted heap.

Undaunted by their strenuous lovemaking, Adam hungrily kissed Connor. Breaking free after several long, wet and satisfying moments, he wrapped his arms around Connor's pliant, sated body. Sitting up against the head of the bed, he pulled Connor into his lap, the smaller man's back snuggled tightly against his chest.

Weak and sated, Connor allowed Adam to gently manhandle him, adrift in the contentment and bliss coursing through his body with every rapid thud of his pounding heart. He felt lethargic and drained, as if all of his physical needs had been completely met in one moment of time. His body nearly unresponsive, Connor's mind was racing, invigorated by the excitement and pleasure of coupling with this raw, powerful man.

He tilted his head and let it drop down onto one of Adam's broad waiting shoulders, luxuriating in the feeling of Adam's warm hands as they massaged his arms and chest.

Nestled between the big man's bulging thighs, Connor wiggled his ass and pressed more comfortably against his lover's still mostly erect cock. Amazed at the man's staying power, he was pleased their lovemaking had been shorter than the last night they spent together. Connor's head still hurt and the travel and tension of the day had drained him.

Relaxing fully against Adam's hot, encompassing frame, Connor felt his eyes start to flutter closed. A slight tugging on his hair made his eyes pop open. He turned his head to look at Adam, but a low grunt and heavy hand on his head halted his movement.

"What are you doing?" The unfamiliar tugging sensation continued, as Adam's hands worked at the side of his head. Suddenly he felt the leather tie slip off from around his neck.

A warm, rich, deep whisper blew seductively past his ear as Adam said, "Finishing the last ritual of our bonding ceremony." A quick, playful bite landed on his neck. "Claiming you again, for all the world to see."

The bite was soothed over with a long, teasing lick of Adam's tongue then the mark was given a gentle kiss. Adam trailed a line of soft, light kisses down Connor's throat and shoulder.

"That tickles!" Adam's touch brought out gooseflesh on Connor's skin. He tried to squirm away, but Adam held him fast and continued the soft kisses until Connor laughed and struggled harder. "Let go, you overgrown Sasquatch!"

Unfazed by the smaller man's escape attempts, Adam held on tightly and heaved them both down flat onto the bed, nestling Connor to his chest, back to front. He threw a confining leg over Connor's and cradled his lover's injured head on his thick arm, wrapping the other arm around Connor's waist.

Once they were settled comfortably under the quilt, Adam nuzzled at the soft flesh behind Connor's ear. "I will never release you." Adam sucked Connor's ear lobe into his mouth and worried it with his teeth. Connor's heart skipped a beat at the faintly troubling words until Adam released his ear and added, "Never release you from my heart, adada. Never ask it of me."

Connor's heartbeat jumped back into a regular rhythm and slowed down to a normal rate. The momentary fear faded. Connor was thrilled with the intensity of feeling Adam's words had left in his heart.

"I won't, ever. I promise you." Connor reached up to brush his hair off his face. His fingers caught on the silver band in his newly braided strands of hair. He instantly rolled the band in his hand and tried to feel the carvings he knew were on it with his fingertips. The metal was heavy and cool to the touch, a bold statement of commitment for all to see. Connor knew from watching the band in Adam's hair, it caught the firelight with the least bit of movement and sparkled with every turn and tilt of the head.

There would be no mistaking who he belonged with. The other natives Connor had seen at the ceremony all had beads or feathers and ties in their hair. None had silver bands, only the alpha leader of the pack and his mate wore them.

Connor felt a swell of pride spread through his chest. He was mated to the alpha male. He belonged to the pack leader. He wondered briefly where the intense, immediate feeling of possessiveness had come from before dismissing it from his sleep-deprived thoughts.

Snuggling down under the quilt, lulled by the warmth of Adam's furnace-hot body and the calming pulse of the man's heart beating reassuringly against his back, Connor closed his eyes and faded off to sleep, finally secure in the arms of the man he loved.

***

Chapter Sixteen

The moon was rising high in the night sky as
Connor awoke. Something had been nagging at him,
insisting he awaken. Connor rolled over onto his back
and blinked the sleep from his eyes, taking in the
changes in the small room.

The cabin was awash in moonlight, the bright,
white beams of ghostly color streaming in from the
solitary window. The fire blazed and crackled, fresh
logs heaped in the hearth. The faint smell of iqemik
drifted in the air along with other scents Connor
couldn't place. If he concentrated, he could hear the
winds whispering through the trees surrounding the
cabin, a low wispy sound as if nature was sighing.

Sitting up, Connor searched for some sign of
Adam, slightly disturbed at waking alone. The wind's
pitch changed and the soft, muted tunes of flutes
touched the farthest limits of his hearing. A creeping
unease made his skin began to crawl when soothing
warmth filled his mind. He instantly knew Adam was
close by and coming to him.

The door to the cabin opened and Adam filled
the threshold, a bowl of food and a pitcher in his hands.
He quickly discarded the robe he had worn outside and
hung it by the door, before striding naked to Connor's
side.

Sitting on the edge of the bed, Adam placed the
bowl filled with cooked meats and biscuits between

them. He smiled at Connor and reached out to ruffle his sleepy lover's hair.

"A gift from the women of the tribe. They say you will need your strength this night." Adam offered a piece of meat to Connor, and then took one for himself and chewed.

Connor reached out and pulled Adam's hand to his mouth, seductively sucking the cooking oils and meat juices from his glistening fingertips.

"They may be right." Connor let a leering smirk tug his lips into a suggestive, challenging smile. "But you'd better eat up, too, big guy. It could get to be a long haul, even for you." He hungrily ate another piece of meat from the bowl and sipped at the water right from the pitcher, suggestively licking his own fingers clean this time.

"I will be interested to see if you can wear me out, adada." Adam leaned forward and bestowed a lingering kiss on Connor's wet, parted mouth. Connor returned the kiss with a growing enthusiasm that Adam cut short when he pulled back slightly.

"Remember, Connor, you will transform for the first time tonight." Adam left one hand cupped around the back of Connor's neck, his fingers combing comfortingly through the longer strands of soft yellow hair, skillfully avoiding the wounds on Connor's scalp. "I will be at your side for all of it, now and each time it happens. It can be painful and startling, but do not fear it. You will be protected in my arms and in my soul. No harm will come to you."

"I trust you, Adam. Otherwise, I wouldn't be here. I love you. I know you'll take care of me."

Connor returned the favor and fed Adam a bite, allowing his fingers to linger over the man's full lips as Adam sucked the tidbit from his hand.

"And I love you. Now and for all time, adada. I have waited too long for you not to cherish and protect every breath you take."

Adam placed another small morsel of food in Connor's mouth. When Connor chewed and swallowed, Adam pulled him near and kissed him deeply, exploring every millimeter of his lips, teeth and soft palate. Connor groaned and moved closer, hands lifting up to knead Adam's broad, satin-smooth shoulders.

Without breaking the kiss, Adam pulled Connor to the edge of the mattress. He slipped off the bed to kneel on the floor between Connor's knees. His hands lightly stroked and soothed over Connor's still sleep-warm flesh, teasing and awakening all the young man's hypersensitive nerves.

Connor arched into the caress, hungrily devouring Adam's mouth, tongues dueling and exploring with total abandon. Passion rose higher and higher with each touch of Adam's callused, knowing hands.

Connor broke away from the kiss to gasp and moan, eager for more than just touching. "God, Adam! I need you, want you in me, on me, buried in me. Now."

Adam soothed over Connor's fevered skin and rained a steady trail of kisses over his face and neck. "Soon, adada, soon. The moon is almost at its crest. The time will be upon us soon."

He continued to kiss his way down Connor's flushed body, paying attention to the taut, rosy nubs peaked high on his chest. Adam suckled at them, one then the other, tugging with his teeth and lightly gnawing at them.

Connor hissed and moaned, his cock filling to full engorgement. He arched into Adam's hold, pressing the man's head more firmly against his chest with both hands. Just when Connor thought his nipples were hot enough they would melt off his body, Adam broke away to lick down the fine trail of golden hair that led from Connor's navel to his groin.

Without warning, Adam pushed Connor's thighs further apart, bent over his engorged cock and swallowed it to the root. He wasted no time on tender foreplay and slow preparation. He sucked hard and bobbed up and down the shaft in a rapid, deep motion, one hand massaging Connor's sac.

Placing a massive hand on Connor's chest, he pushed him down on the bed, bringing Connor's firm, small ass into view. Using one thick finger, Adam rubbed and pressed at the opening to Connor's body, teasing the ring of tight muscle but never breaching it.

The added stimulation at his hole, along with the relentlessly delicious sucking and tugging of his balls sent Connor over the top and he shuddered through his first climax of the night.

"Ugh, god, shit! Adddddam!"

Grabbing Connor by the hips, Adam turned him over and dragged him partially off the bed. Connor's legs were stretched wide, kneeling on Adam's massive thighs. His ass was high in the air, perched on the edge of the mattress in front of Adam's face.

Still in a post-coital haze of bliss, Connor rubbed his cheek against the sleep-warmed quilt under him and concentrated on the sensations ricocheting through his body. The climax had been hard and fast and his brain hadn't caught up with his body's responses yet. In the background, the sound of the flutes grew louder and the soft thud-thud of drums joined in.

Looking over his shoulder into the corners of the room, Connor watched as the shadows stepped away from the walls once more, taking the shape of native warriors. They were cloaked in a variety of animal skins and headdresses, faces painted with streaks of red, brown and white, all of them indistinct. They swayed and pranced in time to the music, rattles punctuating the rhythm in an irregular beat. The more Connor watched, the less frightened he became of the spectacle.

When the figures pulled free of the shadows to dance in the ghostly bright beams of moonlight illuminating the center of the room, he did nothing more than blink to bring them into better focus. They seemed content to dance in the moonlight beyond the reach of the bed.

Glancing back at Adam, who appeared unperturbed by the sudden presence of the ghostly apparitions, Connor relaxed against the quilt again, a feeling of security and peace flowing over him with each soothing stroke of Adam's hands over his back and hips.

Closing his eyes, Connor lost himself in the sensation of Adam's heavy, seductive touch. He gasped and rubbed his reviving cock against the quilt. His pushed his ass higher in the air as Adam kneaded the firm globes of his butt, spreading his cheeks wide. The cooler air of the room wafted over the sensitive flesh and Connor shivered. The shiver turned to a low moan when Adam's hot, wet tongue ran up the length of his cleft.

Adam teased at the puckered hole, smothering it with broad, slick swipes, then traced the deep cleft up to the tip of Connor's tailbone. He repeated the slow teasing again and again until Connor writhed and pushed back against his tongue, seeking more.

His knees still rested on Adam's thick thighs and their sweaty skin made Connor's balance unstable. He twisted his hands into the bed quilt and groaned into its folds as Adam jabbed at the tight ring of muscle of his ass with the tip of his tongue. Each slick, wet jab of the long, thick muscle inflamed his nerve ends. Each insistent thrust breached his opening a little farther, leaving behind a droplet of slick saliva, the tongue stroking the tight ring and coaxing it to relax.

Drawing in a deep breath and slowly letting it out, Connor felt the ring loosen and Adam's tongue delve deeper in an immediate response. Connor tried to shove his ass back and impale himself on the twisting, teasing muscle, but the strong hands holding open his cheeks held him pinned in place against the bed. Connor moaned and surrendered himself to the sweet torture, eager for whatever Adam wanted to do to him.

Once Connor relaxed, Adam shoved his tongue in deeper and licked at the walls of his channel, tongue lapping in long, sinewy strokes that made Connor flail and scream into the mattress.

Out There in the Night

Moonlight filled the room as the moon rose toward its peak in the night sky. The dancers whirled, streams of white, hazy beams lancing through their shadowy figures, giving substance and a ghostly glow to the thin, dark specters.

Moving in time to the increasing tempo of the drums, Adam removed one hand from Connor's ass to stroke his own full erection several time, gathering some of the viscous fluids his body secreted and using them to lubricate his cock.

Allowing the change from man to werewolf to overtake him, Adam continued rimming Connor's ass. He used his agile canine tongue to reach up higher into Connor and to stroke deeper.

Connor bucked and heaved under Adam's increasing weight, the sudden, repeated, forceful laps over his prostate overwhelming his senses. Adam's thighs grew wider and coarse hair appeared under Connor's knees. The hot fingers digging into his flesh felt like superheated, callused pads of sandpaper and the low, seductive grunts that had been coming from Adam now turned into low, thrilling growls of primal lust.

Aware of what was happening, but too distracted to concentrate on what it meant to him, Connor rode the building crest of his impending climax to the top of the wave. Lights flashed behind his eyes and heat soared through his body, melting nerve paths along the way. Connor hung in a haze of delicious bliss, suspended in time. Even the rough, impaling force of Adam sheathing himself to the root in his relaxed and fluttering ass didn't pull Connor back from the surreal plane of blissful abandon.

When he did finally crash back to earth, Connor found himself being ridden hard, his ass smashed tightly against Adam's furred groin, bristled hairs grinding against the opening to his body, inflaming him and stirring his spent cock back to life.

Adam's arms had been planted on either side of Connor's head. They were now replaced with the stout forearms of a wolf, the sharp claws spread on the quilt by Connor's head.

The long tongue that had been exploring the inside of his ass was licking up his spine and nuzzling at his neck. Teeth nipped at his shoulders. Strong jaws clamped around his neck and a playful growl rumbled in his ears as he was roughly shaken.

Pressure inside his asshole told Connor that Adam's climax was building. He pushed back, impaling himself deeper.

Cock fully engorged and held firmly in place inside Connor by the thick bulb at the base, Adam began a brutal series of rapid-fire thrusts, pounding Connor against the edge of the bed.

Connor felt a rush of hot liquid against his channel walls, but Adam didn't let up. The pounding rhythm increased until Connor felt his own orgasm building deep in his belly. Every hard thrust and jarring stroke seemed to hit a switch that pushed his pleasure higher, increasing his need and lust. He began shoving back, matching thrust for thrust, and letting loose a groan for each throaty growl Adam uttered.

A sudden, unexpected surge of heat burned through Connor's body, bringing with it a rush of power that left a trail of gooseflesh. Connor gasped and bucked back, his fading stamina oddly renewed. A flash of light caught his eye and Connor turned his face to see a beam of moonlight stretching across the bed, illuminating the both of them. Over his shoulder the fierce face of a huge, black werewolf grinned at him.

As Connor watched, mesmerized, Adam raised his muzzle to point at the night sky and let loose a howl that shook the rafters of the cabin. In response, the shadow dancers whirled in a frenzy of rhythm and the winds rattled the shingles. From outside a chorus of howls echoed Adam's triumphant call and Connor felt something deep inside of him shift and grow.

An odd stretching of his muscles drew Connor's attention to his arms and he watched as soft, pure-white fur rapidly grew to cover his flesh. His bones reshaped themselves and he felt his jaw extend and elongate. His heart raced and his senses tingled. Unbelievable power and strength coursed through his body. He knew he was transforming. Connor Jacy was now a werewolf.

The smells of the room became intense and the scent of his coupling with Adam flared his desire to a painful crest. Growling, he threw himself into the rhythm of passion, reaching over to nip sharply at Adam's forearm, signaling his increasing need.

Adam answered the wordless request by slowing down his thrust, making his strokes longer, putting more pressure on the ring of nerve filled muscle in Connor's ass, heightening Connor's sense of fullness and pleasure.

Despite the increase in pleasure, Connor growled and whined, wanting a quicker path to his orgasm.

A heavy weight descended on Connor's back, as Adam rested his chest against him, pinning him down, holding him immobile, making it clear who was the alpha male and who would set the pace.

Connor snarled, then whined when the thrusts stopped altogether. A slowly sensuous grinding of Adam's hips, pushed the thick cock inside of him higher and Connor felt it pulsing against his cum-coated channel. More hot fluid flooded his insides as Adam arched and ejaculated for the second time, bathing the walls of his ass and stimulating his sensitized prostate. As the last spurt of juices escaped Adam's cock, the rapid thrusts started again and Connor's passions began to rise once more.

Determined to do nothing to slow the arrival of his desperately needed climax, Connor relaxed into the rhythm. Adam had left him little room to maneuver his lower half, so he shoved his hindquarters back into the wild thrusts and clenched his ass tight on the out-stroke, maximizing the pressure at his opening.

The pounding beat jarred his body, roughly rubbing his own bristled sheath up and down his leaking cock against the mattress edge. The sensation was like having a warm, thick hand glide over his shaft. Connor pushed out with his abdominal muscles and managed to add pressure to the tip of his cock each time it escaped the thick, newly-formed sheath of protective flesh.

Suddenly the rapid thrusts slowed and Adam hammered home a series of impossibly deep, long strokes. Connor felt as if he could taste his lover as cum rocketed out of Adam's shaft and up his ass. Connor experienced the overpowering thrill of total sexual satisfaction, his own climax bursting from the hollow of his belly and skating up his arched, sweat-covered spine at the same time as Adam's.

Connor was sure he saw bursts of glitter-like lights explode out of his body and dance in the beams of shimmering moonlight, showering the shadow dancers in a layer of silver dust.

Slumping against the mattress, pinned under Adam's confining embrace, Connor witnessed the shadows merge back into the corners of the room. The sounds of the flutes and drums grew faint on the whispering winds until they were gone, replaced by a joyful howling that was picked up and carried for miles.

Adam added his voice to the chorus, the sound breathtaking and powerful in Connor's ears. Connor instinctively raised his own muzzle in the air and added a new voice to the pack.

Feeling sated and boneless, Connor flexed his new limbs and relaxed, lazily examining all the physiological changes in his body. A playful shake of his neck accompanied by a sharp nip to his ear forced him to focus on his lover.

He could feel Adam's cock shrinking inside of him and Connor clenched his ass to keep the full, delicious sensation for as long as he could.

Adam growled deep in his throat and nuzzled Connor's cheek before withdrawing his shaft completely.

Moonlight now filled the room, beams of the white light landing on the center of the bed. Connor whined and snarled when Adam lifted him off the floor and settled him on the bed. Moonbeams played across his thick, white coat of fur and Connor studied it in amazement.

Adam landed on the bed beside him, suddenly back in human form, a gentle leer on his smiling face.

"Your eyes are still green." Adam touched the side of Connor's fur-covered snout, lovingly stroking over the soft, fine fur. "I had hoped they would remain unchanged after the transformation."

Connor tried to talk, but found his vocal cords were different and nothing but a series of whines escaped. Adam continued petting his face, soothing the sudden panic that gripped him.

"After tonight you will learn to control the change, bend it to your will. You are strong and more beautiful than my visions foretold. Our lodge has been truly blessed by the spirits." Adam wrapped his arms around Connor's still slender form and hugged him close, letting Connor lick his face and lips.

"Tonight we will run as one, and I will teach you the ways of our kind. I will show you what true freedom is and you will know what waits for you outside these walls. We are of one soul and spirit now, mated for all time, children of the moon. Out there in the night lies our entwined destiny. Let me show it to you, adada."

Morphing back into his werewolf shape, Adam sprung from the bed with a beckoning yip to Connor. Nervous, but thrilled and excited by the power and wonderment of the magical transformation of his body and soul, Connor joined his lover.

Out There in the Night

Adam pushed open the cabin door and side-by-side, he and Connor ventured out into the moonlit night, their life and adventures just beginning.

The end

Laura Baumbach